Slaves in Algiers

or,

A Struggle for Freedom

Emergent Texts in American Literature

Stephen Carl Arch, *Series Editor*

A series devoted to the publication of affordable editions of currently vital texts from the American literary canon. Reliably edited and annotated, each edition of an emergent text in American literature provides students of American literary history with a trustworthy guide to a text that, once forgotten, has emerged or re-emerged into our consciousness as a valuable record of America's tangled legacy. Conceiving of "America" as a concept always under discussion, of "texts" as any writing that attempts to intervene in its readers' consciousness, and of "emergent" as a record of what we, now, have re-discovered about ourselves, Copley's *Emergent Texts in American Literature* re-introduces works that are becoming indispensable to the world our students will shape.

ALSO AVAILABLE FROM THE COPLEY SERIES
EMERGENT TEXTS IN AMERICAN LITERATURE:

Running a Thousand Miles for Freedom
Or, The Escape of William and Ellen Craft from Slavery
Edited by John Ernest

A Narrative of
Colonel Ethan Allen's Captivity
Edited by Stephen Carl Arch

Paul Laurence Dunbar's
The Fanatics
Edited by Lisa Long

Anna Cora Mowatt's
Mimic Life
Edited by Jeffrey Richards

Mary Wilkins Freeman's
Pembroke
Edited by Mary Rigsby

FORTHCOMING TITLE:

T. S. Arthur's
Ten Nights in a Bar-Room
Edited by Jon Miller

Emergent Texts in American Literature

Slaves in Algiers

or,

A Struggle for Freedom

Susanna Haswell Rowson

An Edition Prepared by
Jennifer Margulis and Karen M. Poremski

A COPLEY EDITION

Copley Publishing Group
Acton, Massachusetts 01720

For Hesperus and Dexter

Printed in the United States of America

ISBN 1-58390-014-4

Library of Congress Catalog Card Number: 00-103327

Cover photo: Courtesy of the Holt Collection, Boston Public Library

Copley Publishing Group
138 Great Road
Acton, MA 01720
800.562.2147 • FAX 978.263.9190
e-mail: textbook@copleypublishing.com
www.copleypublishing.com

Contents

Introduction

Susanna Haswell Rowson (1762–1828) was an extraordinary woman. In a time when few women were known publicly, Rowson became a famous novelist, playwright, actress, and schoolmistress. A prolific writer, she wrote novels, plays, and poetry as well as education manuals and arithmetic primers. Born in England but raised in America, Rowson was a teenager in America during the Revolution. She traveled back to Britain with her Loyalist father when she was sixteen years old. Although she published her first novels in England (*Victoria* appeared in 1786, *Mary; or, the Test of Honour* in 1789), Rowson returned to America in 1793. She lived the remainder of her life in the United States, where, in addition to being an actress and an editor, she became a well-established author. Despite the importance of her writing in early America, however, Rowson is now remembered almost exclusively for her best-selling novel of seduction, *Charlotte Temple* (1791).

Slaves in Algiers; or, A Struggle for Freedom (1794) is Rowson's first and only extant play. Set in Barbary—on the Mediterranean Coast of North Africa—the play follows the lives of several European-American slaves who plot their escape and eventually attain their freedom. One of the main characters is an American woman, Rebecca Constant, who is enslaved by a treacherous, greedy, and poorly spoken Jew, Ben Hassan. Coincidentally, Rebecca's husband and her daughter, Olivia, from whom she has been separated for fourteen years, have also been captured and enslaved in Algiers. In Act I we learn that Rebecca's friends have sent her enough money to ransom herself and several other

Christian slaves, but Ben Hassan intercepts the money and hides it from her. The play also relates the predicaments of two American men, Henry and Frederic, also captive in Algiers; Henry is Olivia's long-lost sweetheart, whereas Frederic is a hapless bachelor who laments his inability to attract women. The cast is rounded out by secondary characters such as Selima, Zoriana, and Sebastian, a drunken Spaniard who helps to free the Americans. Frederic and Fetnah flirt with an attachment, and poor Sebastian thinks he is wooing a woman, but she turns out to be Ben Hassan, who has disguised himself as a woman to hide from the wrath of the Dey[1] of Algiers.

The play's ending, much as in a Shakespearean comedy, neatly reunites Rebecca's lost family. The white American slaves prove virtuous and victorious. Although the details of the play, including the unlikely ending, are fictitious, the play was based on historical events unfolding in post-Revolutionary America. During the late eighteenth and early nineteenth centuries, the Barbary States threatened American commerce, enslaved American seamen, and wounded American pride. As a British colony, America had enjoyed the protection of the British Navy. After the Revolution, however, the American shipping industry lost the protection of the British Navy. For the first time, the Barbary States posed a genuine threat to American business. America's vessels were subject to corsair raids, and American seamen were captured. In June 1793 an Algerine rowboat pursued the crew of an American schooner, the *Lark*, and on the 25th of August another American sea vessel was reportedly taken by the Algerines (Barnaby 105). In both of these assaults on American ships in the Spanish Mediterranean, the captain and crew managed to escape. But by the fall of 1793 the United States learned that the Algerine corsairs had enslaved dozens of American seamen from other ships. Accurate numbers of the European-Americans captured during this period are difficult to ascertain, but most historians agree that over a hundred captives were taken.

[1] This and other foreign terms are explained in the footnotes to the play itself, beginning on page 5.

The fate of the Barbary captives was foremost in the minds of American citizens. Publisher and printer Mathew Carey, in his *A Short Account of Algiers* (1794), explains that "When the news of the misfortune of so many of our citizens arrived in America, the sympathy of the public was excited to the highest possible degree" (36). The problem of European-American slavery reached such a crisis in the late eighteenth century that a consular dispatch from 4 April 1794, reads, "I have lately travell'd through the N. England States, the Generall Topick was the times but principally the Sufferings of our Citizens among the Algerines" (as quoted in Rejeb, 58).

Most Americans believed that the British encouraged the pirates to pillage American ships and enslave American seamen because of Britain's embarrassment at America's successful revolt. Because of British complicity, the challenge from the Barbary pirates seemed to threaten America's existence as a country independent from Great Britain. Resisting the pirates meant asserting American sovereignty and America's right to nationhood. As the enslavement of European-Americans in Barbary became a crisis of international proportions, American writers recognized that their country's embarrassing position vis-à-vis Barbary undermined American rhetoric about the independence enjoyed by the new nation.

The people of the new nation were not just talking about the captives: they were writing about them as well. Rowson's play, first performed at the Chestnut Street Theatre in Philadelphia in 1794, was also staged in Baltimore, Boston, and possibly New York. *Slaves in Algiers* was one of dozens of other theater productions performed to raise awareness of and evoke sympathy for the enslaved Americans. At the end of the eighteenth century, in addition to plays, American literature saw a flourishing of poems, sermons, novels, histories, geographies, tracts, pamphlets, and newspaper articles about Barbary. Wax museums exhibited displays of Barbary, fireworks celebrated the treaty signed between the Algerines and the Americans, and circuses performed to raise money for the benefit of the captives. Although the literary responses to Barbary varied, all included reflections on the nature of freedom, liberty, power, slavery, race, culture, and individuality.

In 1793, when Susanna Haswell Rowson wrote *Slaves in Algiers*, the stand-off between the United States government and the Supreme Magistrate of Algiers, Dey Hassan Bashaw, had reached a crisis. Setting her play in the Barbary Coast, Rowson capitalized on this public attention. Although she emphasizes her compassion for the unfortunate Americans, Rowson insists that her play is not based on actual events. In the preface to *Slaves in Algiers*, Rowson claims that the plot of her first dramatic effort came only from a literary source and her imagination: "Some part of the plot is taken from the Story of the Captive, related by Cervantes, in his inimitable Romance of Don Quixote, the rest is entirely the offspring of fancy" (6). In addition to being inspired by Cervantes and her own "fancy," Rowson was also aware of public sympathy for the white slaves and public insistence that the American government protect American shipping interests.

Informed by political events unfolding in the new nation, *Slaves in Algiers* also addresses issues of domestic concern: women's place in the new republic. The epilogue presents a conventional apology for any faults the work might contain and boldly argues for women's status. In performances of the play, Rowson herself, having just acted in the part of Olivia, rushes on stage, pauses a moment to catch her breath, and exclaims her apology: "'Bless me! I'm most terrified to death./Yet sure, I had no real cause for fear,/Since none but liberal, generous friends are here./Say, will you kindly overlook my errors?" (77). This conventional apology carries more import than usual. Rowson must answer for having written and performed in a play in which one female character insists, "Nature made us equal with [men] and gave us the power to render ourselves superior" (16).

Traditional women's roles are further challenged by this play, in which the main characters are women, and in which "tho' a woman, [Rowson pleads] the Rights of Man" (9). In the epilogue, Rowson imagines the responses of the women in the audience to the play they have just seen:

"The creature has some sense," methinks you say;
"She says that we should have supreme dominion,
"And in good truth, we're all of her opinion. (77)

Although we can read this passage as comic, these lines were not received favorably by all; at least one critic objected to the play because of its assertion that women have power over men. Pushing the limits of feminine modesty, Rowson's appearance itself was rare for its time. It was not customary to see women speaking in public, and much less about such controversial issues.

In her book *Women of the Republic* (1986), Linda Kerber discusses the idea that women's sphere of influence in the late eighteenth century was the home. Rather than work in the public sphere as politicians, doctors, or judges, women made their mark on society privately: as wives and mothers, as managers of households. The ideal of the Republican Mother—the woman who would fulfill her duties to her nation by teaching her children the proper morals of America—held powerful sway. Despite Abigail Adams's (somewhat humorous) plea in 1776 to her husband in Congress to "Remember the Ladies" and make them equal partners in the new country, the Revolution did not bring large-scale change in women's status. But though women were not permitted an active role in the American Revolution (for example, in the Continental Congress or as soldiers fighting the war), they played a part in it nonetheless. Boycotts of products imported from and taxed by Britain depended on women's support as consumers. Though they did not march against the British, women supplied food, clothing, and care to those who did.

Women's status was a subject of some debate in the Revolutionary and post-Revolutionary period. The American Revolution was inspired by Enlightenment philosophers, whose questioning of the nature of liberty and inalienable human rights seeped into all subjects, including whether and how women could be citizens. Writers such as Mary Wollstonecraft, Thomas Paine, and Judith Sargent Murray questioned women's place in society and pondered the possibilities of more public, visible roles for women. American women writers such as Susanna Rowson,

Judith Sargent Murray, Mercy Otis Warren, and Hannah Webster Foster wrote novels, essays, and plays that commented on the state of women's education, the place of morality in the nation, and the nature of liberty. In much of her writing, Rowson explores the question of what it means to be an American woman. The title of another Rowson play, *The Female Patriot* (1795, no longer extant), suggests that women's rights also informed her other dramatic works. To be sure, women writers like Rowson, Murray, Warren, and Foster were careful to stay within the social bounds of propriety; they did not noisily demand women's right to vote with public protests (as women would later do in the nineteenth century) but, rather, politely inquired into women's place in an enlightened, civilized society. Nevertheless they made daring steps in asserting that women could be patriots and citizens and could have a say in the life of the new nation. Rowson was one such quiet revolutionary.

Rowson earned her living (and supported her husband) through writing and acting. Her most famous novel, which became a best seller in early America, was *Charlotte Temple* (1791). A novel of seduction, *Charlotte Temple* relates the plight of a naive young girl who is duped by a well-meaning but unscrupulous British officer. Promising to marry Charlotte, her seducer Montraville convinces her to accompany him to America. He never fulfills his promise of marriage and Charlotte, pregnant and abandoned, dies in poverty. In her introduction to *Charlotte Temple*, literary critic Cathy N. Davidson recounts how Charlotte Temple's story profoundly affected thousands of American readers; hundreds of them, believing Charlotte's story to be true, visited and wept over her grave (xii–xiv). Though Rowson's novels had a marked effect on the American reading public, and though her works sold well, lax copyright laws and her husband's spending habits kept the Rowsons from enjoying financial comfort. As successful an author as Rowson was by the time she wrote *Slaves in Algiers*, her family nonetheless suffered financial hardships. The Rowsons decided to try to make a living by performing on stage, and in the summer of 1793, they met Thomas Wignell, who had leased the

Chestnut Street Theatre in Philadelphia. When the Rowson family arrived in Philadelphia, a yellow fever outbreak forced them (and Wignell's entire troop of actors) to Annapolis, Maryland, where they performed in December 1793 and January 1794. They were finally able to move to Philadelphia, America's premier city at the time, where the Chestnut Street Theatre opened in February 1794. In addition to *Slaves in Algiers*, the company also mounted productions that year of original works by American authors, famous British eighteenth-century plays (such as *School for Scandal* and *The Rivals*), and the perennial favorite of audiences, Shakespeare. The works by Shakespeare staged by the company that year included *As You Like It*, *Macbeth*, *Othello*, *Hamlet*, *Merchant of Venice*, *Richard III*, *Romeo and Juliet*, *Cymbeline*, and *Catharine and Petruchio* (a version of *The Taming of the Shrew*). Rowson was undoubtedly influenced by these British plays, as well as by Miguel de Cervantes's *Don Quixote*, which she directly credits.

Because she and her family labored under financial difficulty during this period, it would be fair to assume that Rowson wrote with a popular audience in mind. That Rowson chose the subject of white slavery in Africa for her first attempt at drama, then, suggests the immediacy, urgency, and interest of this subject during the early 1790s. And given that many more Americans attended the theater than read books, Rowson's play further illustrates that the American people, not just negotiating politicians and the enslaved captives themselves, felt a keen interest in Barbary.

Rowson's Americanization of the story of white enslavement anticipated the fascination American drama would have with the United States' skirmishes in the Barbary region. There are a surprising number of early-nineteenth-century plays that address the plight of Barbary captives. David Everett's *Slaves in Barbary* appeared in an anthology entitled *The Columbian Orator* in 1797. James Ellison's *The American Captive, or the Siege of Tripoli*, performed in Boston in 1811 and published in 1812, depicts the treatment of American slaves in Tripoli. Ellison's play was revised by two other playwrights: Jonathon S. Smith, whose version was performed in 1823, and J. S. Jones, whose play was performed in

1841. Mordecai Manuel Noah's *The Siege of Tripoli* was performed first at the Park Theater in May 1820 and later in Philadelphia under the title *Yuseff Caramalli*. John Howard Payne's *Two Galley Slaves* (1822) and *Fall of Algiers* (1825) and Richard Penn Smith's *The Bombardment of Algiers* (1829) are also among the American dramas about Barbary.

As much as *Slaves in Algiers* influenced subsequent American drama, it also borrowed some of the conventions of a Barbary captivity narrative. Barbary captivity narratives, which some scholars classify as closely related to popular and widely-read Indian captivity narratives, are first-person accounts of slavery in the Barbary Coast written by freed white slaves. These narratives, already common in Europe, became an important part of American letters at the end of the eighteenth century. They include, among many others, *Narrative of the Captivity of John Vandike, who was taken by the Algerines in 1791* (1797), *A Journal, of the Captivity and Suffering of John Foss* (1798), *The History of the Captivity and Suffering of Mrs. Maria Martin* (1800), and *The Loss of the American Brig Commerce* (1815). In his anthology of Barbary narratives, *White Slaves, African Masters* (1999), literary critic Paul Baepler argues that these narratives captivated the same audience as Indian captivity narratives. He explains that "The rise in popularity of the Barbary captivity narrative coincides not only with the growing number of U.S. sailors held in North African bondage . . . but also with the resurgent demand for Indian captivity tales during the revolutionary period" (24).

Indian captivity narratives, which were extremely popular in early America, depict the plight of colonial settlers kidnapped by American Indians. An Indian captivity narrative typically describes Native American Indians descending upon a town, killing villagers and burning buildings, forcibly removing the captive from the town and taking him or her to an Indian village. Once captive, the narrator describes the trials of living among the Indians—in a completely foreign culture—and details his redemption or escape from captivity. These narratives often include vivid descriptions of ritual sacrifices and other violence. Based on the lives of colonial settlers, in times of turmoil between whites and Native Americans, the captivity genre first became popular after King Philip's War (1675–1676). It remained popular well into the nineteenth century, when Indian populations had begun to decline seriously. Mary Rowlandson's *A True History of the Captivity and Restoration of Mrs. Mary Rowlandson* (1682), which describes her experiences as a captive during King Philip's War, was the most popular and most often reprinted Indian captivity narrative. She, like other seventeenth-century captives, interprets her hardship as a test from God and believes her redemption to be proof that God cares for his chosen people, the Puritans. By the eighteenth century, however, the genre had evolved into a form of entertainment that was similar to the early novel. Indian captivity narratives also became rhetorical apologies for westward expansion. Like the Indian captivity narrative, Barbary captivity narratives depict the struggles of the white American captive against his racially different captor, often characterized as savage or barbaric. Both kinds of narratives were used to identify particular values with their "civilized," white audience in an attempt to define the quintessential American and his (or her) superiority over people of other races and nations.

In the late eighteenth and early nineteenth century, as America became independent politically, intellectuals began calling for artistic and literary independence to follow. Noah Webster created an American dictionary, in which he argued the need for a separate dictionary to reflect the unique ways Americans used the English language. In addition to Webster and other public intellectuals, authors such as Philip Freneau, Washington Irving, James Fenimore Cooper, and Ralph Waldo Emerson decreed the need for American works by American authors, written in uniquely American language about American themes. This insistence on a uniquely American literature culminated in Emerson's famous remark in his 1837 "American Scholar" address that "We have listened too long to the courtly muses of Europe." The captivity narrative answered this call, centering as it did on questions of national and racial identity and the nature of freedom.

Along with providing unique American works, authors of the period were also called on to write morally edifying pieces. With the increase in the number of people who were literate and the social changes that led more people to the middle classes (and therefore to more leisure time in which to read) came a worry that the general public's reading material was providing dangerous examples of bad behavior. But authors also wanted to sell books, and people did not want to be preached to—they wanted to be entertained. The same was true of playwrights and their audience: people wanted plays to be entertaining, but critics demanded that they also be morally improving. Part of the debate about entertainment versus edification appeared in print, and it is reflected in Rowson's own novel *Mary; or, The Test of Honour* (1789), in which the main character, Mary Norton, deplores the lack of morality in some theatrical works. Mary, a virtuous, honest, and faithful heroine, enjoys the London theater. She finds it an effective arena to influence the audience's morals, whether positively or negatively. The narrator of Rowson's novel explains that "The Theatres afforded our heroine, as they must every sensible person, a rational pleasure; she was delighted with their comedies, and wept the well-wrought scenes of tragic woe" (Vol. 1, 168). The theater is the place where the audience can potentially find rational and sensible enjoyment. But Mary objects to immoral scenes represented on stage, scenes that "we should blush to see practiced in private life" (Vol. 1, 169). She wonders why all comedies cannot be written in a chaste style. Mary asserts:

> It appears to me highly improper to represent before an audience, the greatest part of which are composed of the youthful of both sexes, scenes of immoral tendency, which may not only be a means of leading them into numerous errors, but may corrupt and vitiate their minds in such a manner as to be an irreparable injury to the rising generation. (Vol. 1, 169)

Mary Newton's philosophy of the theater is one that her author shared. Although uneasy about appearing so often on the public stage, Rowson believed that theater could be both entertaining and morally uplifting. In Rowson's philosophy of literature, the stage becomes a place where the American people can learn about proper behavior.

We must also note, however, that many early American authors claimed that their work was morally valuable, even when it presented material dangerous for its young—especially young female—readers. A number of early American seduction novels, which provided titillating details about premarital sex, incest, and illicit relationships, claimed to be valuable as cautionary examples for their impressionable readers. For example, William Hill Brown's *The Power of Sympathy* (1789) and Hannah Webster Foster's *The Coquette* (1797) both dwell on the lurid details of seduction but claim to be educationally valuable. Although it certainly depicts characters who are to be admired and emulated, *Slaves in Algiers* also provides glimpses of untouchable subjects. The play abounds in intrigue and sensuality. The Barbary Coast is an exotic, dangerous setting. Fetnah, wooed by the Dey, and Rebecca, harassed by Ben Hassan, have the threat of rape hanging over them. The presence of a seraglio suggests sexual intimacies. The sinister Ben Hassan dons women's clothing and becomes the object of another man's lust. And the Dey, a mustachioed swarthy North African, comically and threateningly wields a phallic scimitar.

Slaves in Algiers was the subject of considerable debate in the late eighteenth century. When first published, the play received an acrid critique from William Cobbett, a contemporary of Rowson's and a prolific pamphlet writer. In a pamphlet entitled "A Kick for a Bite" (1795, reprinted in 1796), Cobbett—who used the apt sobriquet Peter Porcupine—objects in bitter terms to Rowson's writing. A Federalist and a British native, Cobbett sharply criticizes the authors of the new nation, Rowson among them. Finding fault in America's general overuse of the word "liberty," Cobbett objects in strident terms to the play's insistence on equality for women. He writes:

> I do not know how it is, but I have a strange misgivings hanging about my mind, that the whole moral as well as political world is going to experience a revolution. Who knows but our present House of Representatives, for instance may be succeeded by members of the other sex? What information might not the democrats and grog-shop politicians expect from their loquacity! I'll engage there would be no secrets then. If the speaker should

> happen to be with child that would be nothing odd to us, who have so long been accustomed to the fight; and if he should lie in during the sessions, her place might be supplied by her aunt or grandmother. (24)

Cobbett sees *Slaves in Algiers* as a harbinger of an unacceptable social revolution. The play prompts him to imagine a society in which women actively participate in the public sphere. Believing that women have no place in politics, Cobbett insists that the female's tendency to gossip, as well as her anatomy, makes any woman unfit for public office. Cobbett's remarks on women's frivolities hint at the disruptive power of the play. He is clearly uncomfortable with what he believes to be the play's suggestion that "the whole moral as well as political world . . . experience a revolution." Cobbett cannot bear Rowson's suggestion that women be actors on the political stage.

Cobbett was also irritated by the play's unlikely ending, the triumphant takeover by American captives. When *Slaves in Algiers* was being performed, there was no possibility of escape for the American seamen who had been captured by the Barbary corsairs. Preferring to overlook the obvious parallels between the imagined revolution in the play and the actual American Revolution, Cobbett uses the ending to expose the naive credulity of the American public. From his acerbic remarks about American popular preferences, however, it seems that the real target of Cobbett's criticism may not be Rowson or her melodrama. Rather, he maligns what he believes are the inferior taste, faulty sentiments, and ignorance of the American people.

Cobbett's criticism did not go unchallenged. A member of the House of Representatives, John Swanick, took up the battle cry in Rowson's favor by publishing a response entitled *A Rub from Snub* (1795). Asserting that Porcupine "extols his work in proportion to the vacuities of [his] belly" (vi), Swanick accuses him of "mental sterility" (73) and disparages his overly literal and pedantic reading of the play. This contemporaneous criticism illustrates the way in which Rowson's writing became the subject of public, political discourse, as well as the play's ability to elicit vehement negative and positive responses in the eighteenth century. The emotional power of *Slaves in Algiers* is evident in the debate it provoked between Cobbett and Swanick. This emotion, together with Rowson's suggestive writing, her insight about the new nation, her potentially radical thought, and her humor, remains effective over two hundred years later, though the conflict that generated the original story line has been virtually forgotten.

Cobbett's fear of women leading a social revolution probably arises from the fact that the play's women characters are its primary (rather than secondary) focus. The women make the most important proclamations about liberty in the play. Rebecca is the matriarch of this group of women; she is literally a mother but also a role model and tutor to other women. True to her surname, Rebecca Constant is the most level-headed, serious, and reflective character in the play. We learn of Rebecca's perspicaciousness in the first scene of the play when Fetnah, Ben Hassan's daughter, boasts, "it was she, who nourished in my mind the love of liberty, and taught me, woman was never formed to be the abject slave of man. Nature made us equal with them, and gave us power to render ourselves superior" (16). Fetnah speaks these lines about Rebecca's insistence on freedom and personal responsibility before Rebecca herself appears on stage. Rebecca is a teacher, imparting her wisdom to Fetnah in a maternal way, "nourishing" Fetnah's mind though they are both deprived of physical liberty.

Owned by Fetnah's father and the object of his lust, Rebecca nonetheless remains chaste and honorable, representing ideal American womanhood. Her insistence on freedom even in the face of slavery suggests that her character parallels that of the nation. Rebecca, the purveyor of liberty, is the embodiment of "Columbia," the poetical and oratorical name for the United States that Rowson emphasizes throughout *Slaves in Algiers*. Just as the United States struggled for freedom from a colonizing nation, Rebecca struggles for freedom against the Dey's tyranny and Ben Hassan's advances. Rebecca's constancy, personal loyalty, education, thoughtfulness, integrity, purity, moral uprightness, and unadulterated European-American blood offer a model of, in Rowson's conception, the ideal image of the United States. As literary critic Amelia Howe Kritzer also argues, Rebecca and the other women in the play become models of Republican Motherhood (153, 158).

Rebecca first appears on stage reading a book, exuding an air of thoughtfulness. She murmurs aloud from her reading:

> The soul, secure in its existence, smiles
> At the drawn dagger, and defies its point.
> The stars shall fade away, the sun itself
> Grow dim with age, and nature sink in years,
> But thou shall flourish in immortal youth,
> Unhurt, amidst the war of elements,
> The wreck of matter, or the crush of worlds. (18)

The image of a drawn dagger is a direct allusion to Shakespeare's *Macbeth*, which the Chestnut Street Theatre performed in 1794. Macbeth, the protagonist of Shakespeare's tragedy, sees a drawn dagger before him in a hallucination before he summons enough courage to kill King Duncan. Although he does not know whether the dagger he sees is real or merely a "dagger of the mind," he reaches for his dagger and commits the murder. Rowson posits Rebecca's character as a contrast to Macbeth's. Instead of cowering in the face of a dagger blade or drawing it up to commit murder and suicide, Rebecca remains unperturbed. As long as she is sure of her virtue and her faith, she will be calm and secure in the face of adversity.

If Rebecca's character parallels the nation's, her personal life is emblematic of the torn loyalties Rowson (and many others) experienced after the Revolution. Rowson's interest in the situation and sensibilities of people crossing the Atlantic is also suggested by the title of another of her plays, *Americans in England* (1797, no longer extant). A native of New York, Rebecca falls in love with a British officer, whom she marries against her father's wishes. She mentions meeting him "while my brave countrymen were struggling for their freedom" (69). Though she marries a British officer, Rebecca obviously feels connected to Americans in their fight to be free of British rule. In the end, the differences between Americans, Britons, and other Europeans fade in the face of the tyranny of their captors. American wife and son and British husband and daughter are subjected to slavery at the hands of the North

Africans. Ironically, the enslavement of Christians by "foreigners" becomes a vehicle of domestic reunification, both for the Constant family and (potentially) for the American nation.

Her pristine character established, Rebecca speaks one of the serious morals at the end of the play. When the white slaves have successfully overcome their masters, Rebecca cautions them—and the audience—that slavery and Christian ethics are at odds with each other. Spoken by an irreproachable character whose bearing suggests that of the nation's, these anti-slavery lines have particular importance:

> By the Christian law, no man should be a slave; it is a word so abject, that, but to speak it dyes the cheek with crimson. Let us assert our own prerogative, be free ourselves, but let us not throw on another's neck, the chains we scorn to wear. (73)

Rebecca insists that the Americans must not enslave their African masters in retaliation. If she herself offers the new America a model, then her closing statement may be read as a political message for the United States: We must not emulate our barbarian enslavers but instead teach them a more just and upright way to behave.

At the same time, Rebecca evokes sympathy for her message by putting it in the context of the white Christian. When she cries that the word *slavery* is so shameful that "to speak it dyes the cheek with crimson," Rebecca explicitly connects concerned Christianity with the white European body. Throughout the play it is the white characters who are honest and truthful in their conduct. Contrasted with Rebecca's constancy is Ben Hassan's lasciviousness. He first tells Rebecca that "I be your very good friend" (19) but quickly makes his true wishes more explicit in an aside: "Ah! you be very sly rougue—you pretend not to know how I loves you" (20). Hassan tries to tempt Rebecca with promises of luxury: "You shou'd forget your Christian friends, for I dare say they have forgot you.—I vill make you my vife, I vill give you von, two, tree slaves to vait on you" (21). Duly astonished, Rebecca reminds Hassan that he is already married. Hassan, however, has a ready reply: "our law gives us great many vives.—our law gives liberty in love; you are an American and you must love liberty" (21). Hassan's train of thought from Rebecca as American to American as lover of liberty to American as liberated in love reads comically. At the same time, Rowson uses Hassan's licentiousness to show that "liberty" has only specific meanings and cannot be applied to all aspects of life.

Rebecca replies severely to Hassan's advances, illustrating her moral probity and underscoring her role as a woman of the new nation and an upholder of national values: "Hold, Hassan; prostitute not the sacred word by applying it to licentiousness; the sons and daughters of liberty take justice, truth, and mercy, for their leaders, when they list under her glorious banners" (21). When Rebecca demands that Hassan not prostitute the word *liberty*, she personifies it, converting "Liberty" into a Woman and insisting on that woman's chastity. Liberty is not only chaste, she is a mother. She generates the sons and daughters of America who follow the virtuous path of justice, truth, and mercy. Rebecca creates a matrilineal America, one that begins with a woman and results in upright daughters. Rowson's feminization of America, then, transfers the affairs of the state and the traditional realms of men into the hands of women.

Hassan, on the other hand, is treacherous; he has been berating Rebecca for her ransom money, insisting that her friends in the United States have forgotten her, while all along he has the money in his pocket. From licentious assaults on Rebecca, Hassan then turns to commit further evil by betraying the escaping American slaves. Claiming to help the Americans hire a boat, Hassan reveals his true nature in treacherous asides, heard clearly by the audience. When Frederic reiterates that he will pay no more than two thousand sequins, Hassan underscores his love of money and lack of fidelity and replies, "Den I vill be satisfied with dat, it will be in some measure reward for me—(aside) for betraying you" (23). When Frederic reaffirms that Hassan will purchase a vessel for the Americans' escape, Hassan answers, "I will do every thing that is necessary—(aside) for my own interest" (23). Although only the audience hears the asides, Frederic treats him with suspicion, making an alternate plan for Hassan's inevitable betrayal. As a Jew, Hassan is inherently untrustworthy before he even exhibits his treachery.

Hassan's treachery toward the Americans is paralleled by his duplicity toward his own religion. When Frederic asks him why he wears a turban, Hassan replies (in song) with the story of his boyhood. He reveals that he has been dishonest since his youth in London when he misrepresented the wares he sold on the street and lent out money at fifty percent interest. In the song, Hassan also admits that he made his fortune by counterfeiting the handwriting of cashiers at the bank. His song continues: "Oh! I began to tremble at every gibbet that I saw;/But I got on board a ship, and here was safely landed,/In spite of the judges, the counsellors, attorneys, and the law" (24). Wily enough to escape all of the rules of civilized society, Hassan has one more conversion to make. He turns to Islam because "'twas the safest way" (25). This history of his childhood and early manhood puts Hassan in the worst light. He can remain faithful to nothing and to no one. He follows no law, appears to abandon his religion, and cheats customer and bank clerk alike. He sells his own daughter and intends to betray the Americans. Ben Hassan makes Shylock, the treacherous and exacting Jew in Shakespeare's *The Merchant of Venice* (which the Chestnut Street Theatre also staged in 1794), look angelic.

Hassan is marked as an outsider not only by his lack of moral character but also by his speech. Whereas Rebecca speaks proper upper-class, grammatical English, Ben Hassan has a heavy Yiddish accent, expresses himself in English as a non-native speaker, and has a peculiar sense of grammar. He often (but not always) pronounces "w" as "v," following a Yiddish and Germanic linguistic pattern. He combines subject pronouns with infinitives instead of conjugated verbs (e.g., "dat be very bad," "I be your very good friend") or wrongly conjugates verbs by adding an unnecessary final "s" (e.g., "you likes"). He drops letters from words ("tree" for "three") or pronounces words so distinctly that they are difficult to understand (e.g., he says "ish" for yes, "shartingly" for certainly). Not even the Algerine slave traders speak in such marked language. But these speech patterns do more than mark Ben Hassan as different from the other characters. His Yiddish pronunciation would have been familiar to a Pennsylvania audience, where German immigrants were common. This exotic stranger has no place, morally or linguistically, in the new nation. His slurred speech, which provides comic moments, marks him as unintelligent, groveling, and lower-class. Ben Hassan, Rowson implies, is fit for only the rag trade. The play's portrayal of Ben Hassan as a sniveling, conniving Hebrew whose poor grammar, insincerity, and lasciviousness rival his cupidity suggests that Jews pose a threat to American purity and Christian ideals.

In light of Rebecca's comments that "no man should be a slave," Frederic's closing commentary about Ben Hassan is particularly disturbing: "your avarice, treachery and cruelty should be severely punished; for if any one deserves slavery, it is he who could raise his own fortune on the miseries of others" (73). Explicitly espousing liberty and an end to the enslavement of human beings, Rowson nonetheless implies that slavery would not be an unduly harsh punishment for the Jew.

At the end of the play, the treacherous Dey admits to the barbarous faults of his nation and promises to amend them. Muley Moloc tells the Christian company in his penultimate speech, "I fear from following the steps of my ancestors I have greatly erred" (74). He then concludes, "Henceforth I shall reject all power but such as my united friends shall think me incapable of abusing" (74). Whereas the Dey promises to reform his practices and to learn from his mistakes, Hassan can only repeat, "Oh! that I was but crying old cloaths, in the dirtiest alley in London" (74). Unlike the Dey, he shows no evidence of repentance or sorrow over his misdeeds; he can only pity himself for his misfortunes. His desire to return to his trade of peddling rags, a profession historically associated with Jews, is pathetic.

The complete treachery of Hassan's character underscores a fear of Jewry as well as a xenophobia toward non-Anglo immigrants to the United States. According to Irving J. Sloan, by the American Revolution, when Rowson was an adolescent, the estimated 2,000 Jews in the United States represented a distinct minority (4). Although Jews provided a major source of funding for the American Revolution, they were regarded as spiritually bankrupt, clannish, roguish, and conspiratorial. In his book *A History of the Jews in America,* historian Howard M. Sachar explains, "In the early decades of the new republic, Jews remained at best an object of curiosity, more commonly of faint distrust or distaste" (28). The faint distrust or distaste that many European-Americans felt toward the Jews turns into serious reservations about their place in society in Rowson's play. Even Fetnah, Ben Hassan's daughter, foregoes returning to America with the freed captives. Showing filial duty toward her father, she decides to stay with him in Algiers. Her decision could be a sign that Fetnah has become Rebecca's protégé and has absorbed American ideals to such an extent that she could not imagine abandoning her father. But her show of filial piety can also be read in another way. Although capable of learning America's values, Fetnah, who is half Jewish, might also sully the nation with her presence. In either case, however, Rowson's vision of the morality, integrity, and freedom of the new nation, embodied in Rebecca Constant, is an exclusionary one. The play's anti-Semitic, anti-immigrant components suggest that Rowson believed, like others of her time, that the influx of Jews and other non-Anglo immigrants could only weaken the United States.

Ben Hassan exhibits his treachery through his extreme avarice, and throughout the play Rowson cautions American women against being seduced by riches. A love for material things becomes, in the play's vocabulary, a form of slavery. The Dey's concubines enjoy every luxury: the apartment at the Dey's is "vastly pretty," and Fetnah wears fine clothes. Chosen as the Dey's favorite, Fetnah can expect to be coddled and well treated. The palace comforts of which the young women partake in the opening scene exceed what most of the audience attending the play could have afforded. Despite this wealth, however, Fetnah, presumably echoing Rebecca's insights, insists that wealth and happiness can never be synonymous. She asks Selima,

> Why do you talk of my being a favourite; is the poor bird that is confined in a cage (because a favourite with its enslaver) consoled for the loss of freedom. No! tho' its prison is of gold wire, its food

> delicious, and it is overwhelm'd with caresses, its little heart still pants for liberty . . . . (13)

Fetnah compares her situation to that of a helpless bird's. The irony of enslavement for the bird, as for Fetnah, is that she is caged because she has caught her enslaver's attention: her beauty makes her a desirable possession. Fetnah suggests that male sexual attention is potentially disastrous, leading to a loss of liberty for women.

Fetnah's lines—that is, Rebecca's offstage teachings—carry with them a double meaning. Fetnah has literally been sold by her father to the Dey, bartered like a commodity. Ostensibly deploring her future standing as the Dey's concubine, Fetnah implicitly criticizes the role of European-American women in Western, not Algerine, society. Conversing with another of the Dey's slaves, Selima, Fetnah insists that women should not be slaves to men even when they are not being held against their will. A daring, energetic, and forthright character, Fetnah risks provoking her master's wrath and disguises herself as a boy in order to escape from the Dey's palace and join the American slaves.

Fetnah's denunciation of spiritual enslavement, as well as physical bondage, is better understood in the context of Rowson's other writing. Most of Rowson's fictional depictions of slavery show Europeans and European-Americans as captives. Although she explicitly mentions her aversion to the African slave trade in several texts, Rowson's over-arching concern is gender relations; she urges that women not ensnare themselves in "prisons of gold wires." Rowson, whose target audience is the European-American woman of social standing, often displaces the site of slavery into the exotic East in order to expose white, middle-class women's shortcomings. Even when the slaves are not Christians, Rowson emphasizes what slavery has to teach Western culture and, especially, women in the West. Her 1791 collection *Mentoria; or, the Young Ladies' Friend*, which was first published in the United States in 1794 (the same year that *Slaves in Algiers* appeared in print), is a book with an explicitly didactic agenda. "Urganda and Fatima," a story in *Mentoria*, was reprinted in the

Young Ladies' Guide (1799) as an example of fine writing (Nason, 41). In it, Rowson tells of Fatima, a shepherd's daughter, whose desires result in enslavement. In this fanciful tale, set in an unidentified yet bountiful Eastern region, Fatima's head is turned by the wealth and luxury of the Vizier's palace. Frantic with envy of Semira, the Vizier's concubine who rests on a bed of roses "clad in all the pomp of eastern magnificence, while two slaves were fanning her to rest" (94), Fatima wishes for splendor, slaves, and a downy bed to replace her labor and hard couch. A fairy, Urganda, grants Fatima her wish, turning her into a lovely virgin who inspires the Vizier's lust. But instead of ease and luxury, Fatima finds only unhappiness:

> [Fatima] now thought herself the happiest among the happy; but the Vizier was passionate, capricious, jealous, and extremely cruel, and it was not long before the disappointed Fatima discovered that to be the favorite to the grand Vizier, was to live only in *splendid slavery*. (97, our emphasis)

Fatima's fault—one that many of Rowson's tragic characters make—is to equate wealth with happiness. But wealth and luxury without freedom and moral probity, according to Rowson, are nothing more than slavery. Before learning her lesson, Fatima lusts for wealth a second time. She believes she will find happiness if she becomes Empress of the East. This too fails. Her lord turns out to be deformed and morose, and Fatima finds herself more miserable than before. Because of her lust for wealth, Fatima suffers in splendid slavery, like the Christians in Rowson's other writing who are slaves to greed, avarice, and vice. As the literary precursor to Fetnah in *Slaves in Algiers*, Fatima has built her own cage of gold wires. But Fetnah, taught well by Rebecca, knows that even "splendid slavery" is still slavery, a condition to be deplored.

Like many other authors who wrote about European-American slavery, Rowson uses Algiers as a stage on which to display and boast of the liberty and purity of America. Just as Rowson chose a setting that would capitalize on the American public's immediate interest in Algiers, she also picked a subject that would allow her to comment on women's morality, race, slavery, and freedom. Less interested than other early American writers (including Benjamin Franklin, Royall Tyler, and Peter Markoe) in abolition, Rowson uses the political crisis with Barbary both to criticize and to applaud the nation's women. She insists that American women uphold the highest moral standards and never succumb to "splendid slavery." At the same time, Rowson's play has little to do with the literal slavery promised by its title. Instead of commenting on chattel bondage, Rowson reveals hierarchies of power between men and women. We can only imagine that William Cobbett would be chagrined to know that his much-feared social revolution has taken place and that in the United States, there are now women in Congress whose supposed tendency for gossip and actual lyings-in have not interfered with their abilities to participate in the American political process. Rowson shows herself a visionary, inspiring though imperfect, who anticipates nineteenth-century suffragism and the twentieth-century women's rights movement.

WORKS CITED

Baepler, Paul. *White Slaves, African Masters: An Anthology of American Barbary Captivity Narratives.* Chicago and London: University of Chicago Press, 1999.

Barnaby, H. G. *Prisoners of Algiers: An Account of the Forgotten American-Algerian War 1785–1797.* London: Oxford University Press, 1966.

Carey, Mathew. *A Short Account of Algiers.* Philadelphia, 1794.

Cobbett, William. *A Kick for a Bite; or, Review Upon Review with a critical essay on the works of Mrs. S. Rowson in a letter to the editor or editors of the American Monthly Review.* Second Edition. Philadelphia, printed by Thomas Bradford, 1796.

Davidson, Cathy N. Introduction. *Charlotte Temple.* By Susanna Rowson. New York: Oxford University Press, 1986.

Kerber, Linda K. *Women of the Republic: Intellect and Ideology in Revolutionary America.* New York: Norton, 1986.

Kritzer, Amelia Howe. "Playing with Republican Motherhood: Self-Representation in Plays by Susanna Haswell Rowson and Judith Sargent Murray." *Early American Literature* 31 (1996): 150–66.

Nason, Elias. *A Memoir of Mrs. Susanna Rowson, with Elegant and Illustrative Extracts from her Writings in Prose and Poetry.* Albany, NY: J. Munsell, 1870.

Rejeb, Lofti Ben. "America's Captive Freemen in North Africa: The Comparative Method in Abolitionist Persuasion." *Slavery and Abolition* 9 (1988): 57–71.

Rowson, Mrs. Susanna Haswell. *Mary; or, the Test of Honour.* London, 1789.

———. *Mentoria; or, the Young Ladies' Friend.* Philadelphia, 1794.

Sachar, Howard M. *A History of the Jews in America.* New York: Alfred A. Knopf, 1992.

Sloan, Irving J. *The Jews in America 1621–1977. A Chronology and Fact Book.* Second Edition. New York: Oceana Publications, 1978.

Swanick, John. *A Rub from Snub; or a Cursory Analytical Epistle, Address to Peter Porcupine, Author of the Bone to Gnaw, Kick for a Bite, &c. &c. Containing Glad Tidings for the Democrats, and a Word of Comfort to Mrs. S. Rowson. Wherein the Said Porcupine's Political, Critical and Literary Character is Fully Illustrated.* Philadelphia, 1795.

Suggestions for Further Reading

Allison, Robert. *The Crescent Obscured: The United States and the Muslim World, 1776–1815.* New York: Oxford University Press, 1995.

Baepler, Paul, ed. *White Slaves, African Masters: An Anthology of American Barbary Captivity Narratives.* Chicago and London: The University of Chicago Press, 1999.

Barnaby, H. G. *Prisoners of Algiers: An Account of the Forgotten American-Algerian War, 1785–1797.* London: Oxford University Press, 1966.

Davidson, Cathy N. *Revolution and the Word.* New York and Oxford: Oxford University Press, 1986.

Kerber, Linda K. *Women of the Republic: Intellect and Ideology in Revolutionary America.* New York: Norton, 1986.

Meserve, Walter J. *An Emerging American Entertainment: The Drama of the American People to 1828.* Bloomington: Indiana University Press, 1977.

Parker, Patricia L. *Susanna Rowson.* Boston: G. K. Hall, 1986.

Sachar, Howard M. *A History of the Jews in America.* New York: Alfred A. Knopf, 1992.

Weil, Dorothy. *In Defense of Women: Susanna Rowson (1762–1824).* University Park and London: Pennsylvania State University Press, 1976.

A Note on the Text

The Copley edition of Susanna Haswell Rowson's *Slaves in Algiers* is taken from the first edition of the play, which was published in 1794 by Wrigly and Berriman. The long "s" has been eliminated throughout, and obvious typographical errors have been corrected. Otherwise, we have made every effort to remain faithful to Rowson's late-eighteenth-century language and style, and the text has not been modernized. Typographical oddities have been preserved. The original spelling, punctuation, capitalization, and italicization of the first edition remain.

Inside View of the New Theatre, Philadelphia.

Courtesy, American Antiquarian Society

SLAVES IN ALGIERS

OR, A

STRUGGLE FOR FREEDOM:

A PLAY,

INTERSPERSED WITH SONGS,

IN THREE ACTS.

BY MRS. ROWSON.

AS PERFORMED

AT THE

NEW THEATRES,

IN

PHILADELPHIA AND BALTIMORE.

PHILADELPHIA:

PRINTED FOR THE AUTHOR, BY WRIGLEY AND BERRIMAN, N°. 149, CHESNUT-STREET.

M,DCC,XCIV.

TO

THE CITIZENS OF THE

UNITED STATES

OF

NORTH AMERICA,

THIS FIRST DRAMATIC

EFFORT

IS INSCRIBED,

BY

THEIR OBLIGED FRIEND,

AND HUMBLE SERVANT,

S. ROWSON.

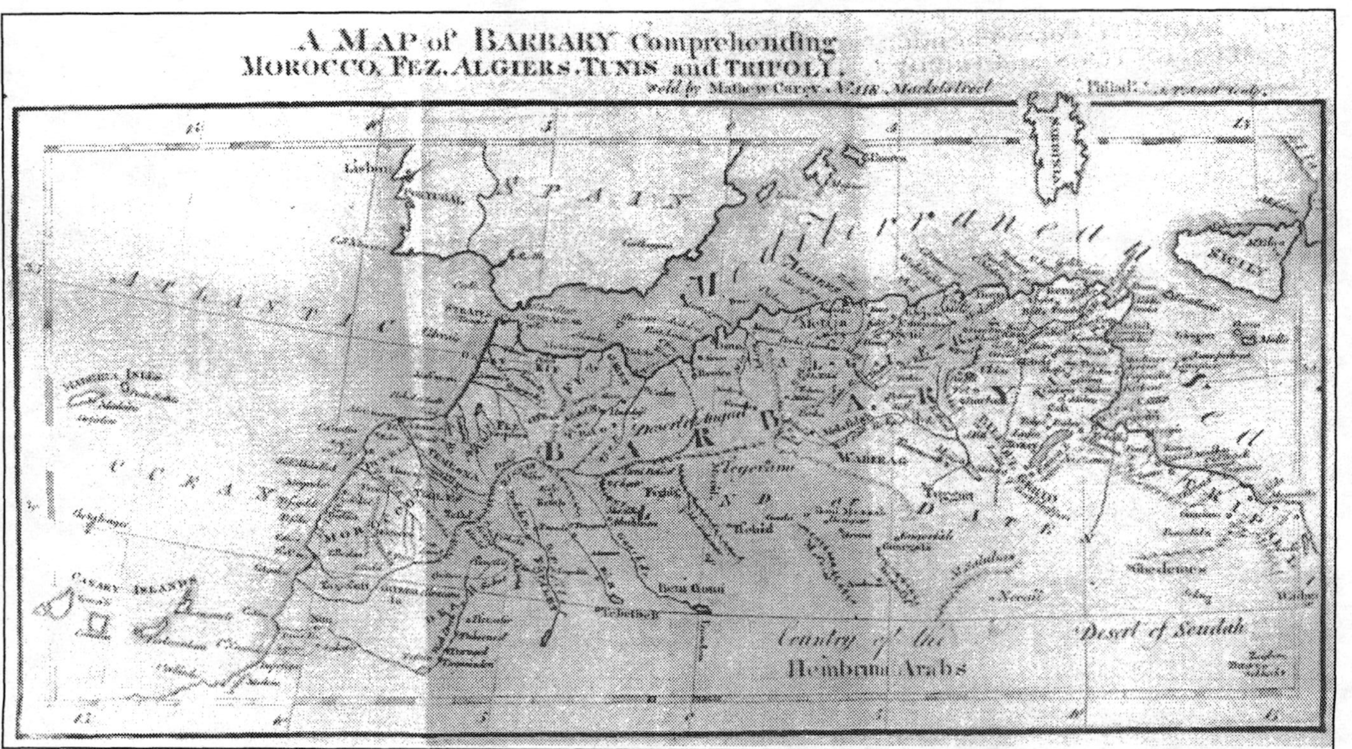

Frontispiece: *A Short Account of Algiers* by Mathew Carey (Philadelphia, 1794). Courtesy, American Antiquarian Society.

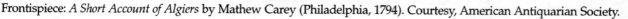

PREFACE

IN offering the following pages to the public, I feel myself necessitated to apologize for the errors which I am fearful will be evident to the severe eye of criticism.

The thought of writing a Dramatic Piece was hastily conceived, and as hastily executed; it being not more than two months, from the first starting of the idea, to the time of its being performed.

I feel myself extremely happy, in having an opportunity, thus publicly to acknowledge my obligation to Mr. Reinagle,[1] *for the attention he manifested, and the taste and genius he displayed in the composition of the music. I must also return my thanks to the Performers, who so readily accepted, and so ably supported their several characters: Since it was chiefly owing to their exertions, that the Play was received with such unbounded marks of approbation.*

Since the first performance, I have made some alterations; and flatter myself those alterations have improved it: But of that, as well as of its merits in general, I am content to abide the decision of a candid and indulgent Public.[2]

1 Alexander Reinagle was a resident of Philadelphia who was also a musician and a Mason. He oversaw the construction of the Chestnut Street Theatre and co-managed it with Thomas Wignell. He wrote the music for the company's productions, including *Slaves in Algiers*.

2 *Slaves in Algiers* was performed first on June 30, 1794, at the Chestnut Street Theatre in Philadelphia, and again, with alterations, on December 22, 1794. Other performances followed in Baltimore, Boston, and possibly New York.

Some part of the plot is taken from the Story of the Captive, related by Cervantes, in his inimitable Romance of Don Quixote, the rest is entirely the offspring of fancy.[3]

I am fully sensible of the many disadvantages under which I consequently labour from a confined education; nor do I expect my style will be thought equal in elegance or energy, to the productions of those who, fortunately, from their sex, or situation in life, have been instructed in the Classics, and have reaped both pleasure and improvement by studying the Ancients in their original purity.

My chief aim has been, to offer to the Public a Dramatic Entertainment, which, while it might excite a smile, or call forth the tear of sensibility, might contain no one sentiment, in the least prejudicial, to the moral or political principles of the government under which I live. On the contrary, it has been my endeavour, to place the social virtues in the fairest point of view, and hold up, to merited contempt and ridicule, their opposite vices. If, in this attempt, I have been the least successful, I shall reap the reward to which I aspire, in the smiles and approbation of a Liberal Public.

[3] Miguel de Cervates Saavedra (1547–1616), the author of *Don Quixote* (1605, 1615), spent five years in slavery in Algiers. In one of the many stories embedded in the novel, a Christian relates his adventures as a captive in Algiers. The Captive sees a handkerchief on the end of a cane held out a window one day and, through many weeks of communication rendered slow and difficult by a language barrier and secrecy, learns that the window is that of Hadji Murad, whose only daughter has become a Christian through the teachings of her father's Christian slave. The daughter, Zoraida, is the one whose white hand holds out the cane with the handkerchief attached, which is filled with money and notes to the Captive. Zoraida wishes to leave her home and go to a Christian land, and she promises riches and her hand in marriage to the Captive if he will help her. Through the handkerchief, she passes him enough money to ransom himself and his fellow captives. Along with a Christian renegade, they help Zoraida escape. After the minor disasters of being cursed by her father and caught by pirates (who steal their money), they finally land in Spanish territory and are reunited with the Captive's family. Among the elements borrowed from Cervantes by Rowson are the intriguing white hand emerging from the cloistered walls of the Algerine household, the Christian whose cover story upon being caught in the garden is that he is picking herbs for a salad, and the slave whose teachings inspire her Muslim pupil to leave her own home and religion.

PROLOGUE

To the New Comedy of SLAVES IN ALGIERS

Written and Spoken by MR. FENNELL.

When aged Priam, to Achilles' tent
To beg the captive corse of Hector went,
The silent suppliant spoke the father's fears,
His sighs his eloquence—his prayers his tears,
The noble conqueror by the sight was won,
And to the weeping sire restor'd the son.[4]

No great Achilles holds *your* sons in chains,
No heart alive to friends' or father's pains,
No generous conqueror who is proud to shew,
That valor vanquish'd is no more his foe;—
But one, whose idol, is his pilfer'd gold,
Got, or by piracy, or subjects sold.
Him no fond father's prayers nor tears can melt,
Untaught to feel for, what he never felt.

What then behoves it, they who help'd to gain,
A nation's freedom, feel the galling chain?
They, who a more than ten year's war withstood,
And stamp'd their country's honor with their blood?
Or, shall the noble Eagle see her brood,
Beneath the pirate kite's fell claw subdu'd?[5]

[4] In the last book of *The Iliad*, Priam goes to the enemy camp to beg his son Hector's body from Achilles, who has been dragging it outside the city walls behind his chariot. Achilles is so impressed by Priam's courage and grief that he surrenders the body for a proper burial.

[5] In the late eighteenth century, the kite (a bird) was a symbol for a rapacious person, one who preys on others; the eagle, of course, was the symbol for America.

View her dear sons of liberty enslaved,
Nor let them share the blessings which they sav'd?
—It must not be—each heart, each soul must rise,
Each ear must listen to their distant cries,
Each hand must give, and the quick sail unfurl'd,
Must bear their ransom to the distant world.

Nor *here* alone, Columbia's sons be free,[6]
Where'er they breathe there must be liberty.
—There *must*! there *is*, for he who form'd the Whole,
Entwin'd blest freedom with th' immortal *soul*.
Eternal twins, whose mutual efforts fan,
That heavenly flame that gilds the life of man,
Whose light, 'midst manacles and dungeons drear,
The sons of honor, must forever cheer.

What tyrant then the virtuous heart can bind?
'Tis vices only can enslave the mind.
Who barters country, honor, faith, to save
His life, tho' free in person, is a slave.
While he, enchain'd, imprison'd tho' he be,
Who lifts his arm for liberty, is free.

To-night, our author boldly dares to chuse,
This glorious subject for her humble muse;
Tho' tyrants check the genius which they fear,
She dreads no check, nor persecution *here*;
Where safe asylums every virtue guard,
And every talent meets its just reward.

Some say—the Comic muse, with watchful eye,
Should catch the reigning *vices* as they fly,[7]

[6] Derived from the name Columbus, Columbia became the poetical name for America in the late eighteenth century.

[7] Thalia, one of the nine Greek muses, gave inspiration to comic dramatists. From the earliest Greek comedies, humor was used to lampoon vices current in the society.

Our author boldly has revers'd that plan,
The reigning *virtues* she has dar'd to scan,
And tho' a woman, plead the Rights of Man.[8]

Thus she, with anxious hope her fate abides,
And to your care, the tender plant confides,
Convinc'd you'll cherish what to freedom's true;
She trusts its life, to candor and to you.

[8] For Rowson's audience, this phrase probably evoked the eighteenth-century debate on the nature of government, most notably expressed by Thomas Paine's *The Rights of Man* (1791). Paine, defending the French Revolution, argues that people in a society assent to their government for the purpose of defending themselves. If the government transgresses upon their individual rights, it violates this contract and justifies revolt.

DRAMATIS PERSONAE[9]

MEN.

MULEY MOLOC, *(Dey of Algiers,)*		Mr. Green.
MUSTAPHA,		Mr. Darley, jun.
BEN HASSAN, *(a Renegado,)*		Mr. Francis.
SEBASTIAN, *(a Spanish Slave,)*		Mr. Bates.
AUGUSTUS,	*(American Captives,)*	Master T. Warrell.
FREDERIC,		Mr. Moreton.
HENRY,		Mr. Cleveland.
CONSTANT,		Mr. Whitlock.
SADI,		Master Warrell.
SELIM,		Mr. Blissett.

WOMEN,

ZORIANA,	*(Moriscan[10] Women,)*	Mrs. Warrell.
FETNAH,		Mrs. Marshall.
SELIMA,		Mrs. Cleveland.
REBECCA,	*(American Women,)*	Mrs. Whitlock.
OLIVIA.		Mrs. Rowson.

Slaves—Guards, &c.

9 All of the actors named here were regular performers at the Chestnut Street Theatre. Note that the part of Olivia was played by Rowson herself; she was said to be an "agreeable singer." Also in the cast were Mr. Bates, who was known for playing low-comedy parts; Mr. Francis, who was famous for his pantomime and created many dances for the company; and Mrs. Whitlock, an actress distinguished for her tragic roles.

10 Moriscan means Moorish, i.e., of or pertaining to the Moors. Early american authors often used *Moriscan* or *Moorish* as adjectives to refer to North Africans.

SLAVES IN ALGIERS;

OR, A

STRUGGLE FOR FREEDOM.

ACT I.—SCENE I

Apartment at the Dey's.[11]

FETNAH and SELIMA.

FETNAH.

Well, it's all vastly pretty, the gardens, the house and these fine clothes; I like them very well, but I don't like to be confined.

SELIMA.

Yet, surely, you have no reason to complain; chosen favorite of the Dey, what can you wish for more.

FETNAH.

O, a great many things—In the first place, I wish for liberty. Why do you talk of my being a favorite; is the poor bird that is confined in a cage (because a favorite with its enslaver) consoled for the loss of freedom. No! tho' its prison is of golden wire, its food delicious, and it is overwhelm'd with caresses, its little heart still pants for liberty: gladly would it seek the fields of air, and even perched upon a naked bough, exulting, carol forth its song, nor once regret the splendid house of bondage.

[11] The Dey was the supreme ruler in Algiers, whose power was absolute. The word *dey* in Turkish means "maternal uncle." The Turkish janissaries who elected the ruler of Algiers called him the dey. They claimed that their father was the Sultan of Turkey, their mother the city of Algiers, and their ruler (or Commander-in-Chief) their mother's brother.

SELIMA.

Ah! But then our master loves you.

FETNAH.

What of that, I don't love him.

SELIMA.

Not love him?

FETNAH.

No—he is old and ugly; then he wears such tremendous whiskers; and when he makes love, he looks so grave and stately, that I declare, if it was not for fear of his huge seymetar,[12] I shou'd burst out a laughing in his face.

SELIMA.

Take care you don't provoke him too far.

FETNAH.

I don't care how I provoke him, if I can but make him keep his distance. You know I was brought here only a few days since—well, yesterday, as I was amusing myself, looking at the fine things I saw everywhere about me, who should bolt into the room, but that great, ugly thing Mustapha. What do you want, said I?—Most beautiful Fetnah, said he, bowing till the tip of his long, hooked nose almost touched the toe of his slipper—most beautiful Fetnah, our powerful and gracious master, Muley Moloc, sends me, the humblest of his slaves, to tell you, he will condescend to sup in your apartment to night, and commands you to receive the high honor with proper humility.

SELIMA.

Well—and what answer did you return.

12 A scimitar is a short, curved, Eastern sword with a single edge used especially among Turks and Persians. In early American writing the scimitar, associated with the exotic East, was often a symbol of Eastern rulers' ruthlessness.

FETNAH.

Lord, I was so frightened, and so provoked, I hardly know what I said, but finding the horrid looking creature didn't move, at last I told him, that if the Dey was determined to come, I supposed he must, for I could not hinder him.

SELIMA.

And did he come?

FETNAH.

No—but he made me go to him, and when I went trembling into the room, he twisted his whiskers and knit his great beetle brows. Fetnah, said he, you abuse my goodness, I have condescended to request you to love me. And then he gave me such a fierce look, as if he would say, and if you don't love me, I'll cut your head off.

SELIMA.

I dare say you were finely frightened.

FETNAH.

Frightened! I was provoked beyond all patience, and thinking he would certainly kill me one day or other, I thought I might as well speak my mind, and be dispatched out of the way at once.

SELIMA.

You make me tremble.

FETNAH.

So, mustering up as much courage as I could; great and powerful Muley, said I—I am sensible I am your slave; you took me from an humble state, placed me in this fine palace, and gave me these rich cloaths; you bought my person of my parents, who loved gold better than they did their child; but my affections you could not buy. I can't love you.—How! cried he, starting from his seat: how, can't love me?—and he laid his hand upon his seymetar.

SELIMA.

Oh, dear! Fetnah.

FETNAH.

When I saw the seymetar half drawn, I caught hold of his arm,—Oh! good my lord, said I, pray do not kill a poor little girl like me, send me home again, and bestow your favor on some other, who may think splendor a compensation for the loss of liberty.—Take her away, said he, she is beneath my anger.

SELIMA.

But, how is it Fetnah, that you have conceived such an aversion to the manners of a country where you were born.

FETNAH.

You are mistaken.—I was not born in Algiers, I drew my first breath in England; my father, Ben Hassan, as he is now called, was a Jew. I can scarcely remember our arrival here, and have been educated in the Moorish religion,[13] tho' I always had a natural antipathy to their manners.

SELIMA.

Perhaps imbibed from your mother.

FETNAH.

No; she has no objection to any of their customs, except that of their having a great many wives at a time.[14] But some few months since, my father, (who sends out many corsairs,) brought home a female captive, to whom I became greatly attached: it was she, who nourished in my mind the love of liberty, and taught me, woman was never formed to be the abject slave of man. Nature made us equal with them, and gave us the power to render ourselves superior.

SELIMA.

Of what nation was she?

[13] Islam.

[14] Under the law of the Koran, a man is permitted to have four wives, provided that he treat them fairly. An unlimited number of female slaves is permitted.

FETNAH.

She came from that land, where virtue in either sex is the only mark of superiority.—She was an American.

SELIMA.

Where is she now?

FETNAH.

She is still at my father's, waiting the arrival of her ransom, for she is a woman of fortune. And tho' I can no longer listen to her instructions, her precepts are engraven on my heart, I feel that I was born free, and while I have life, I will struggle to remain so.

SONG.

I.

The rose just bursting into bloom,
    Admir'd where'er 'tis seen;
Diffuses round a rich perfume,
    The garden's pride and queen.
When gather'd from its native bed,
    No longer charms the eye;
Its vivid tints are quickly fled.
    'Twill wither, droop, and die.

II.

So woman when by nature drest,
    In charms devoid of art;
Can warm the stoic's icy breast,
    Can triumph o'er each heart,
Can bid the soul to virtue rise,
    To glory prompt the brave,
But sinks oppress'd, and drooping dies,
    When once she's made a slave. *Exit.*

SCENE II.

Ben Hassan's house.

REBECCA, (Discovered reading.)

The soul, secure in its existence, smiles
At the drawn dagger, and defies its point.
The stars shall fade away, the sun itself
Grow dim with age, and nature sink in years,
But thou shall flourish in immortal youth,
Unhurt, amidst the war of elements,
The wreck of matter, or the crush of worlds.[15]

[*Lays down the book.*]

Oh! blessed hope, I feel within myself, that spark of intellectual heavenly fire, that bids me soar above this mortal world, and all its pains or pleasures—its pleasures! Oh!—long—long since I have been dead to all that bear the name.—In early youth—torn from the husband of my heart's election—the first only object of my love—bereft of friends, cast on an unfeeling world, with only one poor stay, on which to rest the hope of future joy.—I have a son—my child! my dear Augustus—where are you now?—in slavery.—Grant me patience Heaven! must a boy born in Columbia, claiming liberty as his birth-right, pass all his days in slavery.—How often have I gazed upon his face, and fancied I could trace his father's features; how often have I listen'd to his voice, and thought his father's spirit spoke within him. Oh! my adored boy! must I no more behold his eyes beaming with youthful ardor, when I have told him, how his brave countrymen purchased their freedom with their blood.—Alas! I see him now but seldom; and when we meet, to think that we are slaves, poor, wretched slaves each serving different masters, my eyes overflow with tears.—I have but time to

15 The poem that Rebecca Constant is reading also appears on the frontispiece to Rowson's four-volume novel, *Trials of the Human Heart*, published in the United States in 1795. Rowson probably wrote this poem herself.

press him to my heart, entreat just Heaven, to protect his life, and at some future day restore his liberty.

Enter BEN HASSAN.

BEN HASSAN.

How do you do, Mrs. Rebecca?

REBECCA.

Well, in health, Hassan, but depressed in spirit.

BEN HASSAN.

Ah! Dat be very bad—come, come, cheer up, I vants to talk vid you, you must not be so melancholy, I be your very good friend.

REBECCA.

Thank you, Hassan, but if you are in reality the friend you profess to be, leave me to indulge my grief in solitude, your intention is kind, but I would rather be alone.

BEN HASSAN.

You likes mightily to be by yourself, but I must talk to you a little; I vantsh to know ven you think your ransom vil come, 'tis a long time, Mrs. Rebecca, and you knows.—

REBECCA.

Oh yes, I know, I am under many obligations to you, but I shall soon be able to repay them.

BEN HASSAN.

That may be, but 'tis a very long time, since you wrote to your friends, 'tis above eight months; I am afraid you have deceived me.

REBECCA.

Alas! perhaps I have deceived myself.

BEN HASSAN.

Vat, den you have no friends—you are not a voman's of fortune?

REBECCA.

Yes, yes, I have both friends and ability—but I am afraid my letters have miscarried.

BEN HASSAN.

Oh! dat ish very likely, you may be here dish two or three years longer; perhaps all your life times.

REBECCA.

Alas! I am very wretched. [*weeps.*

BEN HASSAN.

Come, now don't cry so; you must consider I never suffered you to be exposed in the slave market,[16]

REBECCA.

But, my son.—Oh! Hassan; why did you suffer them to sell my child?

BEN HASSAN.

I could not help it, I did all I could—but you knows I would not let you be sent to the Dey, I have kept you in my own house, at mine own expense, [*Aside.*] for which I have been more than doubly paid.

REBECCA.

That is indeed true, but I cannot at present return your kindness.

BEN HASSAN.

Ah! you be very sly rogue—you pretend not to know how I loves you.

REBECCA.

Aside] What means the wretch.

16 Although some slaves were sold privately or given directly to the Dey of Algiers, others were sold at an open-air market. Here Americans would find themselves with slaves of many different nationalities. The slaves, stripped of some of their clothing, would be made to perform physical tasks, and their bodies would be inspected for imperfections.

BEN HASSAN.

You shou'd forget your Christian friends, for I dare say they have forgot you.—I vill make you my vife, I vill give you von, two, tree slaves to vait on you.

REBECCA.

Make me your wife! why, are you not already married?

BEN HASSAN.

Ish, but our law gives us great many vives.—our law gives liberty in love; you are an American and you must love liberty.

REBECCA.

Hold, Hassan; prostitute not the sacred word by applying it to licentiousness; the sons and daughters of liberty, take justice, truth, and mercy, for their leaders, when they list under her glorious banners.

BEN HASSAN.

Your friends will never ransom you.

REBECCA.

How readily does the sordid mind judge of others by its own contracted feelings; you, who much I fear, worship no deity but gold, who could sacrifice friendship, nay, even the ties of nature at the shrine of idolatry, think other hearts as selfish as your own;—but there are souls to whom the afflicted never cry in vain, who, to dry the widow's tear, or free the captive, would share their last possession.—Blest spirits of philanthropy, who inhabit my native land, never will I doubt your friendship, for sure I am, you never will neglect the wretched.

BEN HASSAN.

If you are not ransomed soon, I must send you to the Dey.

REBECCA.

E'en as you please, I cannot be more wretched than I am; but of this be assured; however depressed in fortune, however sunk in adversity, the soul secure in its own integrity will rise superior to its enemies, and scorn the venal wretch, who barters truth for gold. [*Exit.*

BEN HASSAN—Solus.

'Tis a very strange voman, very strange indeed; she does not know I got her pocket-book, with bills of exchange in it; she thinks I keep her in my house out of charity, and yet she talks about freedom and superiority, as if she was in her own country. 'Tis dev'lish hard indeed, when masters may not do what they please with their slaves. Her ransom arrived yesterday, but den she don't know it—Yesh, here is the letter; ransom for Rebecca Constant, and six other Christian slaves; vell, I vill make her write for more, she is my slave, I must get all I can by her. Oh, here comes that wild young Christian, Frederic, who ransom'd himself a few days since.

Enter FREDERIC.

FREDERIC.

Well, my little Israelite, what are you muttering about; have you thought on my proposals, will you purchase the vessel and assist us?

BEN HASSAN.

Vat did you say you wou'd give me?

FREDERIC.

We can amongst us, muster up two thousand sequins,[17] 'tis all we have in the world.

BEN HASSAN.

You are sure you can get no more?

FREDERIC.

Not a farthing more.

[17] The sequin, or sultanin, was a Turkish coin. Two thousand sequins was worth about nine hundred pounds sterling. A farthing is ¼ penny.

BEN HASSAN.

Den I vill be satisfied with dat, it will in some measure reward me—(*aside*) for betraying you.

FREDERIC.

And you will purchase the vessel.

BEN HASSAN.

I will do every thing that is necessary—(*aside*) for my own interest.

FREDERIC.

You have convey'd provision to the cavern by the sea side, where I am to conceal the captives, to wait the arrival of the vessel.

BEN HASSAN.

Most shartingly, I have provided for them as—(*aside*) as secure a prison as any in Algiers.

FREDERIC.

But, are you not a most extortionate old rogue, to require so much, before you will assist a parcel of poor devils to obtain their liberty.

BEN HASSAN.

Oh! Mr. Frederic, if I vash not your very good friend, I could not do it for so little; the Moors are such uncharitable dogs, they never think they can get enough for their slaves, but I have a vasht deal of compassion; I feels very mush for the poor Christians; I should be very glad—(*aside*) to have a hundred or two of them my prisoners.

FREDERIC.

You would be glad to serve us?

BEN HASSAN.

Shartingly. (*Aside*) Ven I can serve myself at the same time.

FREDERIC.

Prithee, honest Hassan, how came you to put on the turban?

BEN HASSAN.

I'll tell you.

*SONG.[18]

Ven I vas a mighty little boy,
    Heart-cakes I sold and pepper-mint drops;
Wafers and sweet chalk I used for to cry;
    Alacumpeine and nice lolly-pops,

The next thing I sold vas the rollers for the macs
    To curl dere hair, 'twas very good;
Rosin I painted for sealing wax,
    And I forg'd upon it vel brand on vast houd.

Next to try my luck in the alley I vent,
    But of dat I soon grew tir'd and wiser.
Monies I lent out at fifty per cent,
    And my name was I. H. in the Public Advertiser.

The next thing I did was a spirited prank,
    Which at one stroke my fortune was made;
I wrote so very like the cashiers of the bank,
    The clerks did not know the difference, and the monies
        was paid

So, having cheated the Gentiles, as Moses commanded,
    Oh! I began to tremble at every gibbet[19] that I saw;
But I got on board a ship, and here was safely landed,
    In spite of the judges, counsellors, attorneys, and law.

*This song was not written by Mrs. Rowson. [author's note]

18 Ben Hassan's song is filled with street slang. He recounts hawking his wares on the streets of London and cheating his customers. Instead of sealing wax, for example, he would sell rosin (a substance made from distilled turpentine) painted to resemble wax.

19 Gallows.

FREDERIC.

And so to complete the whole, you turn'd Mahometan.

BEN HASSAN.

Oh 'twas the safest way.

FREDERIC.

But Hassan, as you are so fond of cheating the gentiles, perhaps you may cheat us.

BEN HASSAN.

Oh no! I swear by Mahomet.

FREDERIC.

No swearing, old Trimmer,[20] if you are true to us, you will be amply rewarded, should you betray us, (*sternly*) by heaven you shall not live an hour after.—Go, look for a vessel, make every necessary preparation; and remember, instant death shall await the least appearance of treachery.

BEN HASSAN.

But I have not got monies.

FREDERIC.

Go, you are a hypocrite; you are rich enough to purchase an hundred vessels, and if the Dey knew of your wealth—

BEN HASSAN.

Oh! dear Mr. Frederic, indeed I am very poor, but I will do all you desire, and you vill pay me afterwards. (*Aside*—Oh, I wish I could get you well paid with the bastinado.[21]

[*Exit.*

20 A "Trimmer" was someone who changed his loyalty to suit the needs of the moment.

21 The bastinado was a particularly cruel form of punishment sometimes used against slaves and criminals in Algiers. The victim's ankles would be attached by ropes to a pole that was then lifted onto the shoulders of two men. The victim's exposed feet were then cudgeled with thick sticks while he dangled upside down. Afterwards, vinegar was sometimes poured onto the victim's wounds.

FREDERIC—Solus.

I will trust this fellow no farther, I am afraid he will play us false—but should he, we have yet one resource, we can but die; and to die in a struggle for freedom, is better far than to live in ignominious bondage.

[*Exit.*

SCENE III.

Another Apartment at the Dey's.

ZORIANA and OLIVIA.

ZORIANA.

Alas! it was pitiful, pray proceed.

OLIVIA.

My father's ill health obliging him to visit Lisbon, we embarked for that place, leaving my betrothed lover to follow us—but e'er we reached our destined port, we were captured by an Algerine corsair, and I was immediately sent to the Dey, your father.

ZORIANA.

I was then in the country, but I was told he became enamoured of you.

OLIVIA.

Unfortunately he did; but my being a Christian has hitherto preserved me from improper solicitations, tho' I am frequently pressed to abjure my religion.[22]

22 A Muslim man could not marry a non-Muslim; a slave or captive had to be converted to Islam before she could marry. However, many non-Muslim women were forced to become the Dey's concubines and live in his harem. That Olivia has not been subjected to this fate has more to do with Rowson's portrayal of the Dey than with Olivia's status as a Christian.

ZORIANA.

Were you not once near making your escape.

OLIVIA.

We were; my father, by means of some jewels which he had concealed in his cloaths, bribed one of the guards to procure false keys to the apartments, but on the very night when we meant to put our plan in execution, the Dey, coming suddenly into the room, surprized my father in my arms.[23]

ZORIANA.

Was not his anger dreadful?

OLIVIA.

Past description; my dear father was torn from me and loaded with chains, thrown into a dungeon, where he still remains, secluded from the cheering light of heaven; no resting place but on the cold, damp ground; the daily portion of his food so poor and scanty, it hardly serves to eke out an existence lingering as it is forlorn.

ZORIANA.

And where are the false keys?

OLIVIA.

I have them still, for I was not known to possess them.

ZORIANA.

Then banish all your sorrow; if you have still the keys, to-morrow night shall set us all at liberty.

OLIVIA.

Madam!

[23] Rowson had previously used the story line of Olivia in her novel *Mary; or, The Test of Honor* (1789) in the character of the Greek slave Semira, who helps others escape her master Hali while sacrificing her own freedom.

ZORIANA.

Be not alarmed sweet Olivia, I am a Christian in my heart, and I love a Christian slave, to whom I have conveyed money and jewels, sufficient to ransom himself and several others; I will appoint him to be in the garden this evening, you shall go with me and speak to him.

OLIVIA.

But how can we release my father.

ZORIANA.

Every method shall be tried to gain admittance to his prison; the Christian has many friends, and if all other means fail, they can force the door.

OLIVIA.

Oh! heavens, could I but see him once more at liberty, how gladly would I sacrifice my own life to secure his.

ZORIANA.

The keys you have, will let us out of the house when all are lock'd in the embraces of sleep; our Christian friends will be ready to receive us, and before morning we shall be in a place of safety; in the mean time, let hope support your sinking spirits.

SONG.

Sweet cherub clad in robes of white,
    Descend celestial Hope;
And on thy pinions, soft, and light,
    Oh bear thy votary up.
'Tis thou can sooth the troubled breast,
    The tear of sorrow dry;
Can'st lull each doubt and fear to rest,
    And check the rising sigh.
        Sweet cherub &c.

Exeunt.

SCENE IV.

A garden—Outside a house, with small high lattices.[24]

HENRY and FREDERIC.

FREDERIC.

Fearing the old fellow would pocket our cash and betray us afterwards, I changed my plan, and have entrusted the money with a Spaniard, who will make the best bargain he can for us; have you tried our friends, will they be staunch?

HENRY.

To a man; the hope of liberty, like an electric spark, ran instantly through every heart, kindling a flame of patriotic ardour. Nay, even those whom interest or fear have hitherto kept silent, now openly avowed their hatred of the Dey, and swore to assist our purpose.

FREDERIC.

Those whose freedom we have already purchased, have concerted proper measures for liberating many others, and by twelve o'clock to morrow night, we shall have a party large enough to surround the palace of the Dey, and convey from thence in safety the fair Zoriana. (*Window opens and a white handkerchief is waved.*)

HENRY.

Soft;—behold the signal of love and peace.

FREDERIC.

I'll catch it as it falls. (*He approaches; it is drawn back.*)

[24] Gardens and homes in the Muslim world were often constructed so that the women inside could see out, but outsiders could not see the women inside. Thus windows were covered with lattices or curtains. Rowson probably took this detail from Cervantes.

HENRY.

'Tis not design'd for you, stand aside. (*Henry approaching; the handkerchief is let fall, a hand waved, and then the lattice shut.*) 'Tis a wealthy fall, and worth receiving.

FREDERIC.

What says the fair Mahometan?

HENRY.

Can I believe my eyes; here are English characters; and, but I think 'tis impossible, I should say this was my Olivia's writing.

FREDERIC.

This is always the way with you happy fellows, who are favorites with the women; you slight the willing fair one, and doat on those who are only to be obtained with difficulty.

HENRY.

I wish the lovely Moor had fixed her affections on you instead of me.

FREDERIC.

I wish she had with all my soul—Moor or Christian, slave or free woman, 'tis no matter; if she was but young, and in love with me, I'd kneel down and worship her. But I'm a poor, miserable dog, the women never say civil things to me.

HENRY.

But, do you think It can be possible that my adorable Olivia is a captive here?

FREDERIC.

Prithee man, don't stand musing and wondering, but remember this is the time for action. If chance has made your Olivia a captive, why, we must make a bold attempt to set her at liberty, and then I suppose you will turn over the fair Moriscan to me. But what says the letter.

HENRY.

(*Reads.*) "As you have now the means of freedom in your power, be at the north garden gate at ten o'clock, and when you hear me sing, you will be sure all is safe, and that you may enter without danger; do not fail to come, I have some pleasant intelligence to communicate." Yes, I will go and acquaint her with the real state of my heart.

FREDERIC.

And so make her our enemy.

HENRY.

It would be barbarous to impose on her generous nature.—What?—avail myself of her liberality to obtain my own freedom; take her from her country and friends, and then sacrifice her a victim to ingratitude and disappointed love.[25]

FREDERIC.

Tush, man, women's hearts are not so easily broken, we may, perhaps, give them a slight wound now and then, but they are seldom or never incurable.

HENRY.

I see our master coming this way; begone to our friends; encourage them to go through with our enterprise: the moment I am released I will join you.

FREDERIC.

'Till when adieu.

Exeunt severally.

[25] Henry's reluctance to corrupt Zoriana contrasts with the willingness of many protagonists of early American novels of seduction to seduce and then abandon the naive young women who fall in love with them. Henry is unwilling to treat Zoriana the way Charlotte Temple, the heroine of Rowson's 1791 novel, was treated by her seducer Montraville, an officer in the British army.

ACT II.—SCENE I.

Moonlight.—A Garden.

ZORIANA and OLIVIA.

ZORIANA.

Sweet Olivia, chide me not; for tho' I'm fixed to leave this place, and embrace Christianity, I cannot but weep when I think what my poor father will suffer. Methinks I should stay to console him for the loss of you.

OLIVIA.

He will soon forget me; has he not already a number of beautiful slaves, who have been purchased, to banish me from his remembrance.

ZORIANA.

True, but he slights them all; you only, are the mistress of his heart.

OLIVIA.

Hark, did you not hear a footstep?

ZORIANA.

Perhaps it is the young Christian, he waits the appointed signal; I think all is safe, he may approach.

SONG.

Wrap't in the evening's soft and pensive shade,
    When passing zephyrs scarce the herbage moves;
Here waits a trembling, fond, and anxious maid,
    Expecting to behold the youth she loves.

Tho' Philomela[26] on a neighbouring tree
Melodious warbles forth her nightly strain;
Thy accents would be sweeter far to me,
Would from my bosom banish doubt and pain.

Then come dear youth, come haste away,
Haste to this silent grove,
The signal's given, you must obey,
'Tis liberty and love.

Enter HENRY.

HENRY.

Lovely and benevolent lady, permit me thus humbly to thank you for my freedom.

OLIVIA.

Oh Heavens, that voice!

ZORIANA.

Gentle Christian, perhaps I have over-stepped the bounds prescribed my sex. I was early taught a love of Christianity, but I must now confess, my actions are impelled by a tenderer passion.

HENRY.

That passion which you have so generally avowed, has excited my utmost gratitude, and I only wish for power to convince you, how much you have bound me to your service.

OLIVIA.

Oh! (*faints.*)

26 In Greek legend, Philomela is the dishonored sister of Procne whose tongue is cut out by Tereus, King of Thrace, so that she will be unable to tell of her rape. Although versions of the legend vary, in all of them when Procne discovers what has happened, she kills her two sons and serves them to her husband. The gods then turn Philomela, Tereus, and Procne into birds. In the Latin tradition, followed by English poets, Philomela becomes a nightingale.

ZORIANA.

What ails my friend, help me to support her; she is an amiable creature, and will accompany us in our flight. She revives; how are you?—Speak, my Olivia.

HENRY.

Olivia, did you say?

OLIVIA.

Yes; Henry, your forsaken Olivia.

HENRY.

Oh my beloved! is it possible that I see you here in bondage; where is your father?

OLIVIA.

In bondage too—but, Henry, you had forgot me; you could renounce your vows and wed another.

HENRY.

Oh no; never for one moment has my thoughts strayed from my Olivia—I never regretted slavery, but as it deprived me of your sweet converse, nor wished for freedom, but to ratify my vows to you.

ZORIANA.—(Aside.)

How? mutual lovers! my disappointed heart beats high with resentment, but in vain; I wish to be a Christian, and I will, tho' my heart breaks, perform a Christian's duty.

HENRY.

Pardon, beauteous lady, an involuntary error. I have long loved this Christian maid; we are betrothed to each other. This evening I obey'd your summons, to inform you, that grateful thanks and fervent prayers, were all the return I could make for the unmerited kindness you have shewn me.

OLIVIA.

Generous Zoriana, blame not my Henry.

ZORIANA.

Think not so meanly of me, as to suppose I live but for myself—that I loved your Henry, I can without a blush avow, but, 'twas a love so pure that to see him happy, will gratify my utmost wish; I still rejoice that I've procured his liberty, you shall with him, embrace the opportunity, and be henceforth as blest—(*aside.*) as I am wretched.

HENRY.

You will go with us.

ZORIANA.

Perhaps I may—but let us now separate;—to morrow, from the lattice, you shall receive instructions how to proceed: in the mean time here is more gold and jewels. I never knew their value, till I found they could ransom *you* from slavery.

HENRY.

Words are poor.

ZORIANA.

Leave us, my heart's oppress'd, I wish to be alone; doubt not the safety of your Olivia; she must be safe with me, for she is dear to *you*.

[*Henry kisses her hand, bows and exit.—They stand sometime without speaking.*]

ZORIANA.

Olivia!

OLIVIA.

Madam!

ZORIANA.

Why are you silent, do you doubt my sincerity!

OLIVIA.

Oh no—but I was thinking, if we should fail in our attempt; if we should be taken.

ZORIANA.

Gracious heaven forbid!

OLIVIA.

Who then could deprecate your father's wrath. Yourself, my Henry, and my dearest father, all, all, would fall a sacrifice.

ZORIANA.

These are groundless fears.

OLIVIA.

Perhaps they are; but yet, I am resolved to stay behind.

ZORIANA.

Do not think of it.

OLIVIA.

Forgive me; I am determined, and that so firmly, it will be in vain to oppose me.—If you escape—the Power who protects you, will also give to me the means of following; should you be taken, I may perhaps move the Dey to forgive you, and even should my prayers and tears have no effect, my life shall pay the forfeiture of yours.

ZORIANA.

I will not go.

OLIVIA.

Yes, gentle lady, yes; you must go with them; perhaps you think it will be a painful task to meet your father's anger; but indeed it will not; the thought of standing forth the preserver of the dear author of my being, of the man who loves me next to heaven, of the friend who could sacrifice her own happiness to mine, would fill my soul with such delight, that even death, in its most horrid shape, could not disturb its tranquility.

ZORIANA.

But, can you suppose your father, and your lover,

OLIVIA.

You must assist my design, you must tell them I am already at liberty, and in a place of safety; when they discover the deception, be it your task, my gentle Zoriana, to wipe the tear of sorrow from their eyes. Be a daughter to my poor father, comfort his age, be kind and tender to him, let him not feel the loss of his Olivia. Be to my Henry, (Oh! my bursting heart) a friend, to sooth him in his deep affliction; pour consolation on his wounded mind, and love him if you can, as I have done.

Exeunt.

SCENE II.

Dawn of day—another part of the garden—with an alcove.

Enter FREDERIC.

FREDERIC.

What a poor unfortunate dog I am; last night I slipped into the garden behind Henry, in hopes I should find some distressed damsel, who wanted a knight-errant, to deliver her from captivity; and here have I wandered through windings, turnings, alleys, and labyrinths, till the Devil himself could not find the way out again: some one approaches—by all that's lovely 'tis a woman—young, and handsome too, health glows upon her cheek, and good humor sparkles in her eye;—I'll conceal myself, that I may not alarm her. *Exit into the alcove.*

Enter FETNAH.

SONG.

Aurora,[27] lovely blooming fair,
Unbarr'd the eastern skies;
While many a soft pellucid tear,
Ran trickling from her eyes.
Onward she came, with heart-felt glee,
Leading the dancing hours;
For tho' she wept, she smil'd to see,
Her tears refresh the flowers.
Phoebus, who long her charms admir'd,
With bright refulgent ray;
Came forth, and as the maid retir'd,
He kiss'd her tears away.

What a sweet morning, I could not sleep, so the moment the doors were open, I came out to try and amuse myself.—'Tis a delightful garden, but I believe I should hate the finest place in the world, if I was obliged to stay in it, whether I would or no. If I am forced to remain here much longer, I shall fret myself as old and as ugly as Mustapha. That's no matter, there's nobody here to look at one, but great, black, goggle-ey'd creatures, that are posted here and there to watch us. And when one speaks to them, they shake their frightful heads, and make such a horrid noise—lord, I wish I could run away, but that's impossible; there is no getting over these nasty high walls. I do wish some dear, sweet, Christian man, would fall in love with me, break open the garden gates, and carry me off.

FREDERIC. (Stealing out.)

Say you so my charmer, then I'm your man.

FETNAH.

And take me to that charming place, where there are no bolts and bars; no mutes and guards; no bowstrings[28] and seymetars.—

[27] Aurora is the Roman goddess of the dawn; the word came to be used to refer not only to dawn but also to the East, the Orient. Phoebus is the personification of the sun as well as the god of poetry and music.

[28] A bowstring was an instrument used to strangle; it was associated particularly with Turks in the eighteenth century.

Oh! it must be a dear delightful country, where women do just what they please.

FREDERIC.

I'm sure you are a dear, delightful creature.

FETNAH.

(*Turning, see's him, and shrieks.*)

FREDERIC.

Hush, my sweet little infidel, or we shall be discovered.

FETNAH.

Why, who are you; and how came you here?

FREDERIC.

I am a poor forlorn fellow, beautiful creature, over head and ears in love with you, and I came here, to tell you how much I adore you.

FETNAH.

(*Aside.*) Oh dear! what a charming man. I do wish he would run away with me.

FREDERIC.

Perhaps this is the lady who wrote to Henry, she looks like a woman of quality, if I may judge from her dress. I'll ask her.—You wish to leave this country, lovely Moor?

FETNAH.

Lord, I'm not a Moriscan; I hate 'em all, there is nothing I wish so much as to get away from them.

FREDERIC.

Your letters said so.

FETNAH.

Letters!

FREDERIC.

Yes, the letters you dropped from the window upon the terrace.

FETNAH.

(*Aside.*) He takes me for some other. I'll not undeceive him, and may be, he'll carry off.—Yes, sir; yes, I did write to you.

FREDERIC.

To me!

FETNAH.

To be sure; did you think it was to any body else?

FREDERIC.

Why, there has been a small mistake.

FETNAH.

(*Aside.*) And there's like to be a greater if you knew all.

FREDERIC.

And, do you indeed love me?

FETNAH.

Yes, I do, better than any body I ever saw in my life.

FREDERIC.

And if I can get you out of the palace, you will go away with me?

FETNAH.

To be sure I will, that's the very thing I wish.

FREDERIC.

Oh! thou sweet, bewitching little———

[*Catching her in his arms.*]

MULEY MULOC.—without.

Tell him, Fetnah shall be sent home to him immediately.

FETNAH.

Oh lord! what will become of us? that's my lord, the Dey—you'll certainly be taken.

FREDERIC.

Yes, I feel the bow-string round my neck already; what shall I do—where shall I hide.

FETNAH.

Stay, don't be frightened—I'll bring you off; catch me in your arms again.
(*She throws herself in his arms as though fainting.*)

Enter MULEY and MUSTAPHA.

MULEY.

I tell thee, Mustapha, I cannot banish the beautiful Christian one moment from my thoughts. The women seem all determined to perplex me; I was pleased with the beauty of Fetnah, but her childish caprice.———

MUSTAPHA.

Behold, my lord, the fair slave you mention, in the arms of a stranger.

FREDERIC.

(*Aside.*) Now, good bye to poor Pil-garlick.[29]

FETNAH.

(*Pretending to recover.*) Are they gone, and am I safe—Oh! courteous stranger, when the Dey my master knows—.

MULEY.

What's the matter, Fetnah; who is this slave?

FETNAH.

(*Kneeling.*) Oh mighty prince, this stranger has preserved me from the greatest outrage.

[29] Frederic, thinking he has been caught by the Dey and is lost, refers to himself. *Poor Pil-garlick* in early American slang signified "poor me." Literally, it means "peeled garlic" and was first applied to liken a bald head (or a bald-headed man) to peeled garlic.

MULEY.

What outrage?

FETNAH.

Now, do not look angry at your poor little slave, who knowing she had offended you, could not rest, and came early into the garden, to lament her folly.

FREDERIC.

(*Aside.*) Well said, woman.

MULEY.

Rise, Fetnah; we have forgot your rashness—proceed.

FETNAH.

So, as I was sitting, melancholy and sad, in the alcove, I heard a great noise, and presently, four or five Turks leap'd over the wall, and began to plunder the garden; I screamed; did not you hear me, Mustapha?

FREDERIC.

(*Aside.*) Well said, again.

FETNAH.

But, the moment they saw me, they seized me, and would have forced me away, had not this gallant stranger run to my assistance—they, thinking they were pursued by many, relinquished their hold, and left me fainting in the stranger's arms.

MULEY.

'Tis well.

MUSTAPHA.

But, gracious sir, how came the stranger here?

FREDERIC.

(*Aside.*) Oh! confound your inquisitive tongue.

MULEY.

Aye, Christian; how came you in this garden?

FETNAH.

He came from my father. Did not you say my father sent you here?

FREDERIC.—[Aside].

[*Bows.*]—Now, who the devil is her father?

FETNAH.

He came to beg leave to gather some herbs for a sallad, while they were still fresh with morning dew.

FREDERIC.

(*Aside.*) Heaven bless her invention!

MULEY.

Go to your apartment.

FETNAH.

Oh dear! if he should ask him any questions when I am gone, what will become of him. *Exit.*

MULEY.

Christian, gather the herbs you came for, and depart in peace.—Mustapha, go to my daughter Zoriana; tell her I'll visit her some two hours hence, 'till when, I'll walk in the refreshing morning air.

Exit Muley and Mustapha.

FREDERIC.—Solus.

Thanks to dear little infidel's ready wit; I breath again—Good Mr. Whiskers I am obliged by your dismission of me—I will depart as fast as I can; and yet I cannot but regret leaving my lovely little Moor behind—who comes here the apostate Hassan.—Now could I swear some mischief was a foot.—I'll keep out of sight and try to learn his business. *Retires.*

Enter BEN HASSAN and MUSTAPHA.

BEN HASSAN.

Indeed, I am vashtly sorry that my daughter has offended my good lord the Dey; but if he will admit me to his sublime presence, I can give him intelligence of so important a nature, as I makes no doubt, will incline him to pardon her, for my sake.

MUSTAPHA.

I will tell him you wait his leisure. *Exit.*

FREDERIC.

The traitor is on the point of betraying us.—I must if possible prevent his seeing the Dey.

[*Runs to Ben Hassan with all the appearance of violent terror.*]

Oh! my dear friend Hassan, for heaven's sake what brought you here; don't you know the Dey is so highly offended with you, that he vows to have you impaled alive.[30]

BEN HASSAN.

Oh dear! Mr. Frederic, how did you know.

FREDERIC.

It was by the luckiest chance in the world; I happened to be in this garden, when I overheard a slave of yours informing the Dey, that you had not only amassed immense riches, which you intended to carry out of his territories; but, that you had many valuable slaves, which you kept concealed from him, that you might reap the benefit of their ransom.

BEN HASSAN.

Oh, what will become of me!—but, come, come; Mr. Frederic, you only say this to frighten me.

[30] Impaling was a form of punishment believed to be common in Algiers. Although it is doubtful that any American slaves were actually impaled alive, accounts of impaling struck terror into Americans and influenced early American writers. Most notably, the protagonist of Royall Tyler's *The Algerine Captive* (1797) witnesses the impaling of a recaptured slave.

FREDERIC.

Well, you'll see that; for I heard him command his guards to be ready to seize you, when he gave the signal, as he expected you here every moment.

BEN HASSAN.

Oh! What shall I do?

FREDERIC.

If you stay here, you will certainly be *bastinadoed—impaled—burnt*.

BEN HASSAN.

Oh dear! Oh dear!

FREDERIC.

Make haste my dear friend; run home as fast as possible; hide your treasure, and keep out of the way.

BEN HASSAN.

Oh dear! I wish I was safe in Duke's Place. *Exit.*

FREDERIC.

Let me but get you once safe into your own house, and I'll prevent your betraying us I'll warrant. *Exit.*

SCENE III.

Fetnah's Apartment.

FETNAH and SELIMA.

FETNAH.

Now will you pretend to say, you are happy here, and that you love the Dey?

SELIMA.

I have been here many years; the Dey has been very good to me, and my chief employment has been to wait on his daughter,

Zoriana, till I was appointed to attend you, to you perhaps, he may be an object of disgust; but looking up to him, as a kind and generous master, to me he appears amiable.

FETNAH.

Oh! to be sure, he is a most amiable creature; I think I see him now, seated on his cushion, a bowl of sherbet by his side, and a long pipe in his mouth. Oh! how charmingly the tobacco must perfume his whiskers—here, Mustapha, says he, "Go, bid the slave Selima come to me"—well it does not signify, that word slave does so stick in my throat—I wonder how any woman of spirit can gulp it down.

SELIMA.

We are accustomed to it.

FETNAH.

The more's the pity: for how sadly depressed must the soul be, to whom custom has rendered bondage supportable.

SELIMA.

Then, if opportunity offered, you would leave Algiers.

FETNAH.

That I would, most cheerfully.

SELIMA.

And perhaps, bestow your affections on some young Christian.

FETNAH.

That you may be sure of; for say what you will, I am sure the woman must be blind and stupid, who would not prefer a young, handsome, good-humored Christian, to an old, ugly, ill natured Turk.

Enter SADI—with robe, turban, &c.

FETNAH.

Well, what's your business?

SADI.

I—I—I—I'm afraid I'm wrong.

SELIMA.

Who sent you here?

SADI.

I was told to take these to our master's son, young Soliman. But some how, in the turnings and windings in this great house, I believe I have lost myself.

SELIMA.

You have mistaken—

FETNAH.

Mistaken—no, he is very right; here, give me the cloaths, I'll take care of them, (*takes them*) there, there, go about your business, it's all very well.—(*Exit Sadi.*) Now, Selima, I'll tell you what I'll do; I'll put these on—go to the Dey, and see if he will know me.

SELIMA.

He'll be angry.

FETNAH.

Pshaw! You're so fearful of his anger, if you let the men see you are afraid of them, they'll hector and domineer finely, no, no, let them think you don't care whether they are pleased or no, and then they'll be as condescending and humble.—Go, go—take the cloaths into the next apartment. (*Exit Selima.*) Now, if by means of these cloaths, I can get out of the palace, I'll seek the charming young Christian I saw this morning, we'll get my dear instructress from my father's and fly, together, from this land of captivity to the regions of Peace and Liberty.

END OF THE SECOND ACT.

ACT III.—SCENE I.

A kind of Grotto.

FREDERIC, HENRY, SEBASTIAN, and SLAVES.

SEBASTIAN.

Now, if you had trusted me, at first, I'll answer for it, I had got you all safe out, aye, and that dear, sweet creature, madam Zoriana too—what a pity it is she's Mahometan, your true bred Mahometans never drink any wine[31]—now, for my part, I like a drop of good liquor, it makes a body feel so comfortable, so—so, I don't know howish, as if they were friends with all the world—I always keep a friend or two hid here, [*takes out some bottles*] mum, don't be afraid, they are no tell tales—only when they are trusted too far.

FREDERIC.

Well, Sebastian, don't be too unguarded in trusting these very good friends to night.

SEBASTIAN.

Never fear me; did not I tell you I'd shew you a place of safety;—well, havn't I perform'd my promise:—When I first discovered this cave, or cavern, or grotto, or cell, or whatever your fine spoken folks may call it; this, said I, would be a good place to hide people in;—so I never told my master.

HENRY.

This fellow will do some mischief, with his nonsensical prate.

FREDERIC.

I don't fear him, he has an honest heart, hid under an appearance of ignorance, it grows duskish, Sebastian, have we good centinals placed at the entrance of the cell?

[31] Drinking alcohol is strictly prohibited by the Koran, which specifies its punishment as eighty lashes.

SEBASTIAN.

Good centinals! why do you suppose I would trust any with that post but those I could depend on?

HENRY.

Two hours past midnight we must invest the garden of the Dey; I have here a letter from Zoriana, which says, she will, at that time be ready to join us—and lead us to the prison of my Olivia's father; Olivia is by some means already at liberty.

CENTINEL—without.

You must not pass.

FETNAH.

No—but I must, I have business.

SEBASTIAN.

What, what, what's all this? *Exit.*

FETNAH.

Nay, for pity's sake, don't kill me. (*Re-enter Sebastian, forcing in Fetnah habited like a boy.*)

SEBASTIAN.

No, no, we won't kill you, we'll only make you a slave, and you know that's nothing.

FETNAH.

(*Aside*) There is my dear Christian, but I won't discover myself, till I try if he will know me.

HENRY.

Who are you, young man, and for what purpose were you loitering about this place.

FETNAH.

I am Soliman, son to the Dey, and I heard by chance, that a band of slaves had laid a plot to invest the palace, and so I traced some of them to this cell, and was just going—

FIRST SLAVE.

To betray us.

SECOND SLAVE.

Let us dispatch him, and instantly disperse till the appointed hour.

SEVERAL SLAVES.

Aye, let us kill him.

HENRY.

Hold; why should we harm this innocent youth.

FIRST SLAVE.

He would be the means of our suffering most cruel tortures.

HENRY.

True, but he is now in our power; young, innocent, and unprotected. Oh my friends! let us not, on this auspicious night, when we hope to emancipate ourselves from slavery, tinge the bright standard of liberty with blood.

SLAVES.

'Tis necessary; our safety demands it.

(*They rush on Fetnah, in her struggle her turban falls off—she breaks from them, and runs to Frederic.*)

FETNAH.

Save me, dear Christian! it's only poor little Fetnah.

FREDERIC.

Save you my sweet little infidel—why, I'll impale the wretch, who should move but a finger against you.

SEBASTIAN.

Oh! Oh! a mighty pretty boy to be sure.

FREDERIC.

But tell me—how got you out of the palace, and how did you discover us.

FETNAH.

I have not time now, but this I will assure you, I came with a full intention to go with you, if you will take me, the whole world over.

FREDERIC.

Can you doubt—

FETNAH.

Doubt, no to be sure I don't; but you must comply with one request, before we depart.

FREDERIC.

Name it.

FETNAH.

I have a dear friend, who is a captive at my father's; she must be released, or Fetnah cannot be happy, even with the man she loves. (*Draws aside, and confers with Henry.*)

SEBASTIAN.

Well, here am I, Sebastian; who have been a slave, two years, six months, a fortnight, and three days, and have, all that time worked in the garden of the Alcaide,[32] who has twelve wives, thirty concubines, and two pretty daughters; and yet not one of the insensible husseys ever took a fancy to me.—'Tis dev'lish hard—that when I go home, I can't say to my honoured father, the barber, and to my reverend mother, the laundress—this is the beautiful princess, who fell in love with me; jumped over the garden wall of his serene holiness her father, and ran away with your dutiful son, Sebastian—then, falling on my knees—thus.

HENRY.

What's the matter, Sebastian? There is no danger, don't be afraid, man.

[32] An Alcaide is a commander of a fortress.

FREDERIC.

Sebastian, you must take a party of our friends, go to the house of Ben Hassan, and bring from thence an American lady. I have good reason to think you will meet with no opposition; she may be at first unwilling to come, but, tell her—friends and countrymen await her here.

FETNAH.

Tell her, her own Fetnah expects her.

FREDERIC.

Treat her with all imaginable respect:—Go, my good Sebastian; be diligent, silent, and expeditious. You, my dear Fetnah, I will place in an inner part of the grotto, where you will be safe, while we effect the escape of Olivia's father.

FETNAH.

What, shut me up!—Do you take me for a coward?

HENRY.

We respect you as a woman, and would shield you from danger.

FETNAH.

A woman!—Why, so I am; but in the cause of love or friendship, a woman can face danger with as much spirit, and as little fear, as the bravest man amongst you.—Do you lead the way; I'll follow to the end. *(Exit Fetnah, Frederic, Henry, &c.)*

SEBASTIAN.

Bravo! Excellent! Bravissimo!—Why, 'tis a little body; but, ecod, she's a devil of a spirit.—It's a fine thing to meet with a woman that has a little fire in her composition. I never much liked your milk-and-water ladies: to be sure, they are easily managed—but your spirited lasses require taming; they make a man look about him—dear, sweet, angry creatures, here's their health. This is the summum-bonum of all good:—If they are kind, this, this, makes them appear angels and goddesses:—If they are saucy, why then, here, here, in this we'll drown the remembrance of the bewitching, froward little devils—in all kind of difficulties and vexations, nothing helps the invention, or cheers the courage, like a drop from the jorum.[33]

SONG.

When I was a poor, little innocent boy,
About sixteen or eighteen years old;
At Susan and Marian I cast a sheep's eye,
But Susan was saucy and Marian was shy;
So I flirted with Flora, with Cecily and Di.
But they too, were frumpish and cold.
Says Diego, one day, what ails you I pray?
I fetch'd a deep sigh—Diego, says I,
Women hate me.—Oh! how I adore 'em.
Pho; nonsense, said he, never mind it, my lad.
Hate you, then hate them boy, come, never be sad,
Here, take a good sup of the jorum.

If they're foolish and mulish, refuse you, abuse you,
No longer pursue,
They'll soon buckle too
When they find they're neglected,
Old maids, unprotected,
Ah! then 'tis their turn to woo;
But bid them defiance, and form an alliance,
With the mirth-giving, care-killing jorum.

I took his advice, but was sent to the war,
And soon I was call'd out to battle;
I heard the drums beat, Oh! how great was my fear,
I wish'd my self sticking, aye, up to each ear

[33] Sebastian's song celebrates the glory of drunkenness. A jorum is a large drinking bowl or vessel as well as its contents, usually some kind of homemade alcoholic punch. Despite the strict laws in Islam prohibiting the consumption of alcohol, Christian slaves sometimes opened taverns in Algiers where they served alcohol to the Christian population and to less scrupulous Muslims.

In a horse-pond—and skulked away to the rear.
When the cannon and bombs 'gan to rattle,
Said I to myself, you're a damn'd foolish elf,
Sebastian keep up, then I took a good sup.
Turkish villains, shall we fly before 'em;
What, give it up tamely and yield ourselves slaves
To a pack of rapscallions, vile infidel knaves,
Then I kissed the sweet lips of my jorum.

No, hang 'em, we'll bang 'em, and rout 'em, and scout 'em.
If we but pursue
They must buckle too:
Ah! then without wonder,
I heard the loud thunder,
Of cannon and musketry too.
But bid them defiance, being firm in alliance,
With the courage-inspiring jorum. *Exit.*

SCENE II.

Ben Hassan's house.

REBECCA and AUGUSTUS.

AUGUSTUS.

Dear mother, don't look so sorrowful; my master is not very hard with me. Do pray be happy.

REBECCA.

Alas! My dear Augustus, can I be happy while you are a slave? my own bondage is nothing—but you, my child.

AUGUSTUS.

Nay, mother, don't mind it; I am but a boy, you know.—If I was a man—

REBECCA.

What would you do my love?

AUGUSTUS.

I'd stamp beneath my feet, the wretch that would enslave my mother.

REBECCA.

There burst forth the sacred flame which heaven itself fixed in the human mind; Oh! my brave boy, [*embracing him*] ever may you preserve that independent spirit, that dares assert the rights of the oppressed, by power unawed, unchecked by servile fear.

AUGUSTUS.

Fear, mother, what should I be afraid of? an't I an American, and I am sure you have often told me, in a right cause, the Americans did not fear any thing.

Enter HASSAN.

HASSAN.

So, here's a piece of work; I'se be like to have fine deal of troubles on your account. Oh! that ever I should run the risque of my life by keeping you concealed from the Dey!

REBECCA.

If I am trouble to you, if my being here endangers your life, why do you not send me away?

BEN HASSAN.

There be no ships here, for you to go in; besides, who will pay me?

REBECCA.

Indeed, if you will send me to my native land, I will faithfully remit to you my ransom; aye, double what you have required.

BEN HASSAN.

If I thought I could depend——

Enter SERVANT.

SERVANT.

Sir, your house is surrounded by arm'd men.

BEN HASSAN.

What, Turks?

SERVANT.

Slaves, sir; many of whom I have seen in the train of the Dey.

BEN HASSAN.

Vhat do they vant?

SERVANT.

One of my companions asked them, and received for answer, they would shew us presently.

SEBASTIAN—without

Stand away, fellow; I will search the house.

REBECCA.

Oh heavens! what will become of me?

BEN HASSAN.

What will become of me? Oh! I shall be impaled, burnt, bastinadoed, murdered, where shall I hide, how shall I escape them.—(*Runs through a door, as though into another apartment.*)

SEBASTIAN—without.

This way, friends; this way.

REBECCA.

Oh, my child, we are lost!

AUGUSTUS.

Don't be frightened, mother, thro' this door is a way into the garden; If I had but a sword, boy as I am, I'd fight for you till I died.

[*Exit with Rebecca.*

Enter SEBASTIAN &c.

SEBASTIAN.

I thought I hear'd voices this way; now my friends, the lady we seek, is a most lovely, amiable creature, whom we must accost with respect, and convey hence in safety—she is a woman of family and fortune, and is highly pleased with my person and abilities; let us, therefore, search every cranny of the house till we find her; she may not recollect me directly, but never mind, we will carry her away first, and assure her of her safety afterwards; go search the rooms in that wing, I will myself, investigate the apartments on this side. [*Exit slaves.*] Well I have made these comrades of mine, believe I am a favored lover, in pursuit of a kind mistress, that's something for them to talk of; and I believe many a fine gentleman is talked of for love affairs, that has as little foundation; and so one is but talked of, as a brave or gallant man, what signifies whether there is any foundation for it or no;—and yet, hang it, who knows but I may prove it a reality, if I release this lady from captivity, she may cast an eye of affection;—may—why, I dare say she will.—I am but poor Sebastian, the barber of Cordova's son, 'tis true; but I am well made, very well made; my leg is not amiss,—then I can make a graceful bow; and as to polite compliments, let me but find her, and I'll shew them what it is to have a pretty person, a graceful air, and a smooth tongue.—But I must search this apartment. *Exit.*

SCENE III.

Another apartment.

Enter BEN HASSAN, with a petticoat and robe on, a bonnet and deep veil in his hand.

BEN HASSAN.

I think now, they vill hardly know me, in my vife's cloaths; I could not find a turban, but this head dress of Rebecca's vill do better, because it vill hide my face—but, how shall I hide my monies: I've got a vast deal, in bills of exchange, and all kinds of paper; if I can but get safe off with this book in my pocket, I shall have enough to keep me easy as long as I live. (*Puts it in his pocket and drops it.*) Oh! this is a judgment fallen upon me for betraying the Christians. (*noise without*) Oh lord! here they come. (*ties on the bonnet, and retires into one corner of the apartment.*)

Enter SEBASTIAN &c.

SEBASTIAN.

There she is, I thought I traced the sweep of her train this way, don't mind her struggles or entreaties, but bring her away.—Don't be alarmed, madam, you will meet with every attention, you will be treated with the greatest respect, and let me whisper to you there is more happiness in store for you, than you can possibly imagine. Friends, convey her gently to the appointed place. (*They take up* HASSAN *and carry him off.*)

BEN HASSAN.

Oh!-o-o-o! *Exit.*

Enter AUGUSTUS and REBECCA.

AUGUSTUS.

See, my dear mother, there is no one here, they are all gone; it was not you, they came to take away.

REBECCA.

It is for you, I fear, more than for myself, I do not think you are safe with me, go, my beloved, return to your master.—

AUGUSTUS.

What, go and leave my mother, without a protector?

REBECCA.

Alas? my love, you are not able to protect yourself—and your staying here, only adds to my distress; leave me for the present; I hope the period is not far off, when we shall never be separated.

AUGUSTUS.

Mother! dear mother!—my heart is so big it almost choaks me.—Oh! how I wish I was a man. *Exit Aug.*

REBECCA—Solus.

Heaven guard my precious child—I cannot think him quite safe any where—but with me, his danger would be imminent; the emotions of his heart hang on his tongue; and the least outrage, offered to his mother, he would resent at peril of his life.—My spirits are oppressed.—I have a thousand fears for him, and for myself—the house appears deserted—all is silent—what's this, [*takes up the pocket-book*] Oh! heaven! is it possible! bills, to the amount of my own ransom and many others—transporting thought—my son—my darling boy, this would soon emancipate you—here's a letter address'd to me—the money is my own—Oh joy beyond expression! my child will soon be free. I have also the means of cheering many children of affliction, with the blest sound of liberty. Hassan, you have dealt unjustly by me, but I forgive you—for while my own heart o'erflows with gratitude for this unexpected blessing, I will wish every human being as happy as I am this moment. *Exit.*

SCENE IV.

Dey's garden.

ZORIANA—Solus.

How vain are the resolves, how treacherous the heart of a woman in love; but a few hours since, I thought I could have chearfully relinquished the hope of having my tenderness returned; and found a relief from my own sorrow, in reflecting on the happiness of Henry and Olivia.—Then why does this selfish heart beat with transport, at the thought of their separation? Poor Olivia—how deep must be her affliction.—Ye silent shades, scenes of content and peace, how sad would you appear to the poor wretch, who wandered here, the victim of despair—but the fond heart, glowing with all the joys of mutual love, delighted views the beauties scattered round, thinks every flower is sweet, and every prospect gay.

SONG.

In lowly cot or mossy cell,
With harmless nymphs and rural swains;[34]
'Tis there contentment loves to dwell,
'Tis there soft peace and pleasure reigns;
But even there, the heart may prove,
The pangs of disappointed love.

But softly, hope persuading,
Forbids me long to mourn;
My tender heart pervading,
Portends my love's return.
Ah! then how bright and gay,
Appears the rural scene,
More radiant breaks the day,
The night is more serene.

Enter HENRY.

HENRY.

Be not alarmed, madam. I have ventured here earlier than I intended, to inquire how my Olivia effected her escape.

ZORIANA.

This letter will inform you—but, early as it is, the palace is wrapp'd in silence, my father is retired to rest—follow me, and I will conduct you to the old man's prison.

HENRY.

Have you the keys?

ZORIANA.

I have;—follow in silence, the least alarm would be fatal to our purpose. *Exeunt.*

[34] Nymphs are semi-divine creatures inhabiting the natural world, and swains are shepherds. In the pastoral tradition, *nymph* and *swain* became the poetic terms for a young maiden and her lover.

SCENE V.

The Grotto again.

SEBASTIAN, leading in BEN HASSAN.

SEBASTIAN.

Beautiful creature, don't be uneasy, I have risked my life to procure your liberty, and will at the utmost hazard, convey you to your desired home: but, Oh! most amiable—most divine—most delicate lady, suffer me thus humbly on my knees to confess my adoration of you; to solicit your pity, and——

BEN HASSAN.

(*In a feigned tone*). I pray, tell me why you brought me from the house of the good Ben Hassan, and where you design to take me.

SEBASTIAN.

Oh! thou adorable, be not offended at my presumption, but having an opportunity of leaving this place of captivity, I was determined to take you with me, and prevent your falling into the power of the Dey, who would, no doubt, be in raptures, should he behold your exquisite beauty.—Sweet, innocent charmer, permit your slave to remove the envious curtain that shades your enchanting visage.

BEN HASSAN.

Oh no! not for the world; I have, in consideration of many past offenses, resolved to take the veil and hide myself from mankind for ever.

SEBASTIAN.

That my dear, sweet creature, would be the highest offense you could commit.—Women were never made, with all their prettiness and softness, and bewitching ways, to be hid from us men, who came into the world for no other purpose, than to see, admire, love and protect them.—Come, I must have a peep under that curtain; I long to see your dear little sparkling eyes, your lovely blooming cheeks—and I am resolved to taste your cherry lips. (*In struggling to kiss him, the bonnet falls off.*) Why, what in the devil's name, have we here?

BEN HASSAN.

Only a poor old woman—who has been in captivity——

SEBASTIAN.

These fifty years at least, by the length of your beard.

FREDERIC—without.

Sebastian—bring the lady to the water side, and wait till we join you.

BEN HASSAN.

I wish I was in any safe place.

SEBASTIAN.

Oh ma'am you are in no danger any where—come make haste.

BEN HASSAN.

But give me my veil again, if anyone saw my face it would shock me.

SEBASTIAN.

And damme, but I think it would shock them—here, take your curtain, tho' I think to be perfectly safe, you had best go barefaced.

BEN HASSAN.

If you hurry me I shall faint, consider the delicacy of my nerves.

SEBASTIAN.

Come along, there's no time for fainting now.

BEN HASSAN.

The respect due—

SEBASTIAN.

To old age—I consider it all—you are very respectable.—Oh! Sebastian what a cursed ninny you were to make so much fuss about a woman old enough to be your grand-mother. *Exeunt.*

SCENE VI.

Inside the palace.

MULEY MOLOC and MUSTAPHA

MULEY.

Fetnah gone, Zoriana gone, and the fair slave Olivia?

MUSTAPHA.

All, dread sir.

MULEY.

Send instantly to the prison of the slave Constant, 'tis he who has again plotted to rob me of Olivia, (*exit Mustapha.*) my daughter too he has seduced from her duty; but he shall not escape my vengeance.

Re-enter MUSTAPHA.

Some of the fugitives are overtaken, and wait in chains without.

MULEY.

Is Zoriana taken?

MUSTAPHA.

Your daughter is safe; the old man too is taken; but Fetnah and Olivia have escaped.

MULEY MOLOC.

Bring in the wretches.—(*Henry, Constant, and several slaves brought in, chained.*)—Rash old man—how have you dared to tempt your fate again; do you not know the torments that await the Christian, who attempts to rob the haram of a Musselman?

CONSTANT.

I know you have the power to end my being—but that's a period I more wish than fear.

MULEY.

Where is Olivia?

CONSTANT.

Safe I hope, beyond your power. Oh! gracious heaven, protect my darling from this tyrant; and let my life pay the dear purchase of her freedom.

MULEY.

Bear them to the torture: who and what am I, that a vile slave dares brave me to my face?

HENRY.

Hold off—we know that we must die, and we are prepared to meet our fate, like men: impotent vain boaster, call us not slaves;—you are a slave indeed, to rude ungoverned passion; to pride, to avarice and lawless love;—exhaust your cruelty in finding tortures for us, and we will smiling tell you, the blow that ends our lives, strikes off our chains, and sets our souls at liberty.

MULEY.

Hence, Take them from my sight;—(*Captives taken off.*)—devise each means of torture; let them linger—months, years, ages, in their misery.

Enter OLIVIA.

OLIVIA.

Stay, Muley, stay—recall your cruel sentence.

MULEY.

Olivia here; is it possible?

OLIVIA.

I have never left the palace, those men are innocent, so is your daughter. It is I alone deserve your anger—then on me only let it fall; it was I procured false keys to the apartments; it was I seduced your daughter to our interest; I bribed the guards, and with entreaty won the young Christian to attempt to free my father; then since I was the cause of their offenses, it is fit my life should pay the forfeiture of theirs.

MULEY.

Why did you not accompany them?

OLIVIA.

Fearing what has happened, I remained, in hopes, by tears and supplications, to move you to forgive my father, Oh! Muley, save his life, save all his friends; and if you must have blood, to appease your vengeance, let me alone be the sacrifice.

MULEY.

Aside.—(How her softness melts me.)—Rise, Olivia—you may on easier terms give them both life and freedom.

OLIVIA.

No—here I kneel till you recall your orders; haste, or it may be too late.

MULEY.

Mustapha, go bid them delay the execution. *Exit Mustapha.*

OLIVIA.

Now teach me to secure their lives and freedom, and my last breath shall bless you.

MULEY.

Renounce your faith—consent to be my wife.—Nay, if you hesitate——

OLIVIA.

I do not—give me but an hour to think.

MULEY.

Not a moment, determine instantly; your answer gives them liberty or death.

OLIVIA.

Then I am resolved. Swear to me, by Mahomet, an oath I know you Musselmen never violate—that the moment I become your wife, my father and his friends are free.

MULEY.

By Mahomet I swear, not only to give them life and freedom, but safe conveyance to their desired home.

OLIVIA.

I am satisfied;—now leave me to myself a few short moments, that I may calm my agitated spirits, and prepare to meet you in the mosque.

MULEY.

Henceforth I live, but to obey you. *Exit.*

OLIVIA.

On what a fearful precipice I stand; to go forward is ruin, shame and infamy; to recede is to pronounce sentence of death upon my father, and my adored Henry. Oh insupportable!—there is one way, and only one, by which I can fulfill my promise to the Dey, preserve my friends and not abjure my faith.—Source of my being, thou can'st read the heart which thou hast been pleased to try in the school of adversity, pardon the weakness of an erring mortal—if rather than behold a father perish;—if, rather than devote his friends to death, I cut the thread of my existence, and rush unbidden to thy presence.—Yes, I will to the mosque, perform my promise, preserve the valued lives of those I love; then sink at once into the silent grave, and bury all my sorrow in oblivion.

Exit.

SCENE VII.

Another apartment.

Enter OLIVIA and MULEY MOLOC.

MULEY MOLOC.

Yes on my life they are free, in a few moments they will be here.

OLIVIA.

Spare me the trial; for the whole world I would not see them now, nor would I have them know at what a price I have secured their freedom.

Enter HENRY and CONSTANT.

CONSTANT.
My child—

HENRY.
My love—

OLIVIA.

My Henry O my dear father?—pray excuse these tears.

Enter MUSTAPHA.

MUSTAPHA.

Great sir, the mosque is prepared, and the priest waits your pleasure.

MULEY.

Come, my Olivia.

HENRY.

The mosque—the priest—what dreadful sacrifice is then intended.

OLIVIA.

Be not alarmed—I must needs attend a solemn rite which gratitude requires—go my dear father—dearest Henry leave me; and be assured, when next you see Olivia, she will be wholly free.

Enter REBECCA.

REBECCA.

Hold for a moment.

MULEY.

What means this bold intrusion?

REBECCA.

Muley, you see before you a woman unused to forms of state, despising titles: I come to offer ransom for six Christian slaves. Waiting your leisure, I was informed a Christian maid, to save her father's life, meant to devote herself a sacrifice to your embraces. I have the means—make your demand of ransom, and set the maid, with those she loves, at liberty.

MULEY.

Her friends are free already;—but for herself she voluntarily remains with me.

REBECCA.

Can you unmoved, behold her anguish;—release her, Muley—name but the sum that will pay her ransom, 'tis yours.

MULEY.

Woman, the wealth of Golconda[35] could not pay her ransom;—can you imagine that I, whose slave she is; I, who could force her obedience to my will, and yet gave life and freedom to those Christians, to purchase her compliance, would now relinquish her for paltry gold; contemptible idea.—Olivia, I spare you some few moments to your father; take leave of him, and as you part remember his life and liberty depends on you. *Exit.*

REBECCA.

Poor girl—what can I do to mitigate your sufferings?

[35] Golconda, now Hyderabad, was an ancient Indian mine celebrated for its diamonds. The name is sometimes used as to mean a "mine of wealth."

OLIVIA.

Nothing—my fate alas! is fixed; but, generous lady—by what name shall we remember you—what nation are you of?

REBECCA.

I am an American—but while I only claim kinship with the afflicted, it is of little consequence where I first drew my breath.

CONSTANT.

An American—from what state?

REBECCA.

New-York is my native place; there did I spend the dear delightful days of childhood, and there alas, I drain'd the cup of deep affliction, to the very dregs.

CONSTANT.

My heart is strangely interested—dearest lady will you impart to us your tale of sorrow, that we may mourn with one who feels so much for us.

REBECCA.

Early in life, while my brave countrymen were struggling for their freedom, it was my fate, to love and be beloved by a young British officer, to whom, tho' strictly forbid by my father, I was privately married.

CONSTANT.

Married! say you?

REBECCA.

My father soon discovered our union; enraged, he spurned me from him, discarded, cursed me, and for four years I followed my husbands fortune, at length my father relented; on a sick bed he sent for me to attend him; I went taking with me an infant son, leaving my husband, and a lovely girl, then scarcely three years old.—Oh heavens! what sorrows have I known from that unhappy hour. During my absence the armies met—my husband fell—my daughter was torn from me; what then avail'd the wealth my dying father had bequeathed me;—long—long did I lose all sense of my misery, and returning reason shewed me the world only one universal blank. The voice of my darling boy first call'd me to myself, for him I strove to mitigate my sorrow; for his dear sake I have endured life.

CONSTANT.

Pray proceed.

REBECCA.

About a year since I heard a rumour that my husband was still alive; full of the fond hope of again beholding him, I, with my son embarked for England; but before we reached the coast we were captured by an Algerine.

CONSTANT.

Do you think you should recollect your husband.

REBECCA.

I think I should—but fourteen years of deep affliction have impaired my memory and may have changed his features.

CONSTANT.

What was his name?—Oh! speak it quickly.

REBECCA.

His name was Constant—but wherefore———

CONSTANT.

It was—it was—Rebecca, don't you know me?

REBECCA.

Alas—how you are altered.—Oh! Constant, why have you forsaken me so long?

CONSTANT.

In the battle you mention, I was indeed severely wounded, nay, left for dead in the field; there, my faithful servant found me, when some remaining signs of life encourag'd him to attempt my recovery, and by his unremitting care I was at length restored; my first returning thought was fixed on my Rebecca, but after repeated inquiries all I could hear was that your father was dead and yourself and child removed farther from the seat of war. Soon after, I was told you had fallen a martyr to grief for my supposed loss.—But see my love, our daughter, our dear Olivia; heaven preserved her to be my comforter.

OLIVIA—(Kneeling and kissing Rebecca.)

My mother, blessed word; Oh! do I live to say I have a mother.

REBECCA.

Bless you my child, my charming duteous girl; but tell me, by what sad chance you became captives?

CONSTANT.

After peace was proclaimed with America, my duty called me to India,[36] from whence I returned with a ruined constitution. Being advised to try the air of Lisbon, we sailed for that place, but Heaven ordained that here in the land of captivity, I should recover a blessing which will amply repay me for all my past sufferings.

Enter MULEY.

MULEY.

Christians you trifle with me—accept your freedom, go in peace, and leave Olivia to perform her promise—for should she waver or draw back—on you I will wreak my vengeance.

[36] Since the establishment of the East India Company in the early seventeenth century, British interests in India had been growing steadily. In the late eighteenth century, troops were called to India, where the British were embroiled in a number of wars with the French and local powers. Upon hearing of the defeat in America, one British official characterized India as possible compensation for the loss of Britain's American colonies: "if it be really true that the British arms and influence have suffered so severe a check in the western world, it is the more incumbent upon those who are charged with the interest of Great Britain in the East to exert themselves for the retrieval of the national loss" (as quoted in P. E. Roberts, *History of British India Under the Company and the Crown*, Delhi and London: Oxford University Press, 1952, p. 193).

REBECCA.

Then let your vengeance fall—we will die together; for never shall Olivia, a daughter of Columbia, and a Christian, tarnish her name by apostasy, or live the slave of a despotic tyrant.

MULEY.

Then take your wish—who's there?

Enter MUSTAPHA—(hastily).

Arm, mighty sir—the slaves throughout Algiers have mutinied—they bear down all before them—this way they come—they say, if all the Christian slaves are not immediately released, they'll raze the city.

REBECCA.

Now! bounteous heaven, protect my darling boy, and aid the cause of freedom.

MULEY.

Bear them to instant death.

MUSTAPHA.

Dread sir—consider.

MULEY.

Vile abject slave obey me and be silent—what have I power over these Christian dogs, and shall I not exert it. Dispatch I say—(*Huzza and clash of swords without.*)—Why am I not obeyed?—(*Clash again—confused noise—several Hazza's,—*)

AUGUSTUS—without.

Where is my mother? save, Oh! Save, my mother.

FREDERIC—speaking.

Shut up the palace gates, secure the guards, and at your peril suffer none to pass.

AUGUSTUS—Entering.

Oh! mother are you safe.

CONSTANT.

Bounteous heaven! and am I then restored to more—much more than life—my Rebecca! my children!—Oh! this joy is more than I can bear.

Enter FREDERIC, FETNAH, SEBASTIAN, BEN HASSAN, SLAVES, &c.

SEBASTIAN.

Great and mighty Ottoman, suffer my friends to shew you what pretty bracelets these are.—Oh, you old dog, we'll give you the bastinado presently.

FREDERIC.

Forbear Sebastian.—Muley Moloc, though your power over us is at end, we neither mean to enslave your person, or put a period to your existence—we are free men, and while we assert the rights of men, we dare not infringe the privileges of a fellow creature.

SEBASTIAN.

By the law of retaliation, he should be a slave.

REBECCA.

By the Christian law, no man should be a slave; it is a word so abject, that, but to speak it dyes the cheek with crimson. Let us assert our own prerogative, to be free ourselves, but let us not throw on another's neck, the chains we scorn to wear.

SEBASTIAN.

But what must we do with this old gentlewoman?

BEN HASSAN.

Oh, pray send me home to Duke's Place.

FREDERIC.

Ben Hassan, your avarice, treachery and cruelty should be severely punished; for, if any one deserves slavery, it is he who could raise his own fortune on the miseries of others.

BEN HASSAN.

Oh! that I was but crying old cloaths, in the dirtiest alley in London.

FETNAH.

So, you'll leave that poor old man behind?

FREDERIC.

Yes, we leave him to learn humanity.

FETNAH—(**Going to Ben Hassan.**)

Very well, good bye Frederic—good bye dear Rebecca: while my father was rich and had friends, I did not much think about my duty; but now he is poor and forsaken, I know it too well to leave him alone in his affliction.

MULEY.

Stay, Fetnah—Hassan stay.—I fear from following the steps of my ancestors, I have greatly erred: teach me then, you who so well know how to practice what is right, how to amend my faults.

CONSTANT.

Open your prison doors; give freedom to your people; sink the name of subject in the endearing epithet of fellow-citizen;—then you will be loved and reverenced—then will you find, in promoting the happiness of others, you have secured your own.

MULEY.

Henceforward, then, I will reject all power but such as my united friends shall think me incapable of abusing. Hassan, you are free—to you my generous conquerors what can I say?

HENRY.

Nothing, but let your future conduct prove how much you value the welfare of your fellow-creatures—to-morrow, we shall leave your capital, and return to our native land, where liberty has established her court—where the warlike Eagle extends his glittering pinions in the sunshine of prosperity.

OLIVIA.

Long, long, may that prosperity continue—may Freedom spread her benign influence thro' every nation, till the bright Eagle, united with the dove and olive-branch, waves high, the acknowledged standard of the world.

THE END

EPILOGUE

WRITTEN AND SPOKEN BY *MRS. ROWSON.*

PROMPTER—behind.

COME—Mrs. Rowson! Come!—Why don't you hurry?

MRS. R.—behind.

Sir I am here—but I'm in such a flurry,
Do let me stop a moment! just for breath,

Bless me! I'm almost terrify'd to death.
Yet sure, I had no real cause for fear,
Since none but liberal—generous friends are here.
Say—will you kindly overlook my errors?
You smile.—Then to the winds I give my terrors.
Well, Ladies tell me—how d'ye like my play?
"The creature has some sense," methinks you say;
"She says that we should have supreme dominion,
"And in good truth, we're all of her opinion.
"Women were born for universal sway;
"Men to adore, be silent, and obey."

True, Ladies—beauteous nature made us fair,
To strew sweet roses round the bed of care.
A parent's heart, of sorrow to beguile,
Cheer an afflicted husband by a smile.
To bind the truant, that's inclined to roam,
Good humour makes a paradise at home.
To raise the fall'n—to pity and forgive:
This is our noblest, best prerogative.
By these, pursuing nature's gentle plan,
We hold in silken chains—the lordly tyrant man.

But pray, forgive this flippancy—indeed,
Of all your clemency I stand in need.
To own the truth, the scenes this night display'd
Are only fictions—drawn by fancy's aid.
'Tis what I wish—But we have cause to fear,
No ray of comfort, the sad bosoms cheer
Of many a Christian, shut from light and day,
In bondage, languishing their lives away.

Say!—You who feel humanity's soft glow,
What rapt'rous joy must the poor captive know;
Who, free'd from slavery's ignominious chain,
Views his dear native land, and friends again?

If there's a sense, more exquisitely fine,
A joy more elevated, more divine;
'Tis felt by those, whose liberal minds conceiv'd,
The generous plan, by which he was reliev'd.

When first this glorious universe began,
And heaven to punish disobedient man;
Sent to attend him, through life's dreary shade,
Affliction—poor dejected, weeping maid.
Then came Benevolence, by all rever'd,
He dry'd the mourner's tears, her heart he cheer'd;
He woo'd her to his breast—made her his own,
And Gratitude appear'd, their first-born son.
Since when, the father and the son has join'd,
To shed their influence o'er the human mind:
And in the heart, where either deign to rest,
Rise transports, difficult to be express'd.
Such, as within your generous bosoms glow,
Who feel return'd, the blessings you bestow.
Oh! ever may you taste, those joys divine,
While Gratitude—sweet Gratitude is mine.